# TRUST

HAVEN SERIES

*Book One*

# LEA HART

D1366493

Dedication

For My Daughters, My Heartbeat


Acknowledgment

I would like to thank Janell Parque for her
editorial wisdom.

*Hang onto your e-readers, I've left nothing out of these romances.*

If you've been craving a small-town romantic dramedy filled with characters that are going to stick with you long after the story ends...look no further. The books from the Haven series are filled with slow-burning romantic escapades, hilarious moments, and a couple of one-two punch to the feels thrown in for good measure.

*Author Warning: The men from the Hawker family are book boyfriend perfection and may induce swooning.*

# TRUST

LEA HART

*Restraint never wrote a love story worth holding on to.*

Mix one grumpy Green Beret with a woman full of positive vibes, add a pile of good intentions, and what do you get? A man praying that his too-happy neighbor finds someone else to annoy so he can get on with his plan to avoid human contact and become the hermit he's meant to be.

Zane Hawker retired from the Army all but broken and is hoping the semi-haunted home he and his brothers have inherited will be the refuge he needs.

Olivia Bennett survived a tragic event in college and vowed to appreciate the blessing by spreading love and light whenever she can, especially to those who think living like a troll under a dark bridge is a good idea.

Sounds like things are about to get interesting in Haven, doesn't it?

Can Zane resist the tornado of gratitude and happiness headed his way? Will Olivia convince her grumpy neighbor that positivity is not rash-inducing, and a little human connection isn't life-threatening?

Are a Ferris wheel and a mongrel dog involved in this
tale of love?
You bet!
It wouldn't be a romantic dramedy, otherwise!
Come see what happens when opposites not only
attract but find a way to trust that happiness comes in
the most unexpected packages.

# CHAPTER ONE

Zane stood on the stone steps of his semi-haunted home and watched the neighbor's dog tear through the grove of trees.

Was one of the family's ghosts hot on its tail? It seemed possible since they'd been more restless than usual.

Crossing his arms, he felt a shiver skitter down his spine and wished he could determine if something fortuitous was on the horizon or something that was going to smash his carefully constructed solitude to smithereens.

The fact that his mind hadn't produced a neutral option, unfortunately wasn't all that surprising. Too many years in the Army had cemented his half-glass-empty mentality and, though a change was due, he didn't think it was imminent. A damn shame since he was about to go mano a mano with Suzy freaking sunshine.

At least that's what he assumed his overly friendly neighbor was since she waved like a maniac whenever he'd passed her in his truck. Why he had to live within walking distance of someone who likely saw the good in everything, he couldn't say. Surely it couldn't have anything to do with God mucking with his plans, could it?

He ran his hand over his neck and let go of the notion because there was no way the Creator had time for the likes of him.

Silently calculating the chances of the woman being slightly horrified when she saw him up close allowed a satisfied smile to form.

*It shouldn't take long to get rid of her.*

Most folks weren't comfortable with the physical scars he'd brought home from his last deployment, and the woman who lived at the end of the lane likely wouldn't be either.

An attitude the head shrinker from the Army would term: unhelpful, unproductive, and unhealthy. He scratched his head and knew several more un-words applied but couldn't seem to muster the enthusiasm to remember them.

Lifting his gaze to the tall trees surrounding the property, he silently thanked his paternal grandmother for leaving him and his brothers the worn-down family homestead. Not only because it was a beautiful broken-down piece of history, but because it allowed him the luxury of living in relative solitude.

Would his neighbor respect his wishes to be left in peace?

The sound of a jangly bike bell rent the air, and he let the question go as a mutt that resembled a small horse skidded to a stop at the bottom of the steps. "Poor you," he murmured, studying the animal that was very nearly as ugly as him.

Not that the dog's looks seemed to matter to the woman who doted on him regularly. Every time he'd seen the two together, there was nothing but mutual admiration and matching silk bows. A thing he thought ridiculous but also weirdly...not nauseating.

He shook his head at the absurd thought, studied the dog's mottled gray hair and paws the size of dinner plates, and decided the red bow tied to its collar wasn't a bad touch.

"Bella, you were supposed to stay close, not run ahead," a light, airy voice called out.

Narrowing his eyes, Zane studied the woman as she got closer and told himself the small bite of physical attraction he experienced every time he caught sight of her was not that big of a deal.

"Hello, neighbor."

Zane lifted his chin in greeting as the woman glided to a stop at the bottom of the stairs and he waited for a look of revulsion once she saw his scars up close. "Morning."

They'd never been closer than a half dozen feet, and he expected that once she got a good look at his face, she'd make some polite conversation and then be gone quickly.

"I can't believe it's taken me a month to catch you at home and won't blame you for thinking me the worst neighbor in the world." She ran her finger over the bell on her bike. "I've made you at least four loaves of chocolate chip banana bread and sadly have to report that Bella and I ate every single one of them when our delivery attempts failed."

"That wasn't..."

"Necessary," she finished. "I know, but I wanted to. After all, we're the only two this far out of town and should stick together." Jumping off the bike, she offered a wide smile. "We've not been properly introduced, but I assume you know that I'm Olivia."

"Yes, I saw it on the mailbox, and..."

"You're Zane Hawker." She adjusted the red bow in her hair and then grabbed a wrapped package out of the bike's basket. "I made it this morning and want you to know that my dog and I did not take one nibble."

"Really..."

"It goes best with tea, but..." Olivia hesitated and tilted her head.

*Here comes the disgust,* he thought as her eyes crawled over his face. Waiting for the imperceptible flinch, he was surprised when nothing but kindness showed in her expression.

"You seem more of a coffee guy, so we'll have that instead. I can go either way as long as there's some caffeine involved."

Did the woman forget her glasses?

Was she legally blind?

There had to be an explanation because there was no way to miss the two-inch red scars bisecting the right side of his face and the burns decorating his neck. He was scary and why this woman wasn't reacting in the typical fashion was...odd. And more unsettling than he could put words to.

Most people slid their eyes away at the first opportunity, but his neighbor was doing the exact opposite. She mounted the stairs with a twinkle in her eyes and handed him a warm foil package that smelled like heaven. "Thank you."

"You're welcome." She stroked her dog's head as it sat on her feet. "And this is Bella, my beautiful girl. She's recently adopted me and doesn't have the whole discipline thing down, so I'll apologize in advance if she does something naughty."

"How exactly does a person get adopted by an animal?" Zane asked, trying to make sense of the woman who was standing well inside his personal space.

"Dogs can choose their family just like people do, and that's what Bella did when she showed up at my house two months ago." She ran her hands over her hair and then winked. "And to answer the unasked question: yes, I did my best to find her family before I claimed her as my own."

"Why didn't you just take her to a shelter?"

A look of horror crossed Olivia's face as she bent down and covered Bella's ears. "Don't even suggest it; she's very sensitive."

Stepping back, he gave the woman a nod and added peculiar to the list of adjectives he'd keep handy to describe her. "Well, I won't keep you, ladies. Thanks for the banana bread."

"You're not keeping us," Olivia said as she looked up at the house. "Aren't you going to invite us in and introduce us to the famous family ghosts?"

"Now isn't a good time, so perhaps another day."

"Why, are they sleeping or something?" she asked with a snort.

"No, but…"

"Great," Olivia replied as she breezed past Zane.

He watched the woman and dog saunter into his sanctuary and tried to come up with a semi-polite way to get rid of them. When Olivia turned in a circle and then gave him a blindingly bright smile, he decided ten minutes of conversation wouldn't kill him.

He just had to make sure that she understood it was a one-time thing.

It shouldn't be all that difficult.

\*\*\*

Olivia stood in the middle of the foyer, letting her eyes travel over the worn wallpaper, exquisite woodwork, and light streaming through the leaded glass windows. "Beautiful."

"What's that?" Zane asked before closing the front door.

"I haven't been inside this house since I was a kid and am both happy and sad to see that nothing much has changed. Are you going to give it some love and bring it back to life?"

"I'm going to restore it if that's what you're asking."

She gave her neighbor a faint smile and wondered why the word love was objectional. Did it have to do with the events that resulted in his scars or possibly an affair of the heart gone wrong?

Whatever the answer, she vowed to find out. A feat that might take a while if Zane's reticence didn't give way before the end of time. Something she wasn't sure that was possible since his scowl was foreboding, his physical presence intimidating, and his energy a pulsing gray.

Not that any of that would stop her.

Running her hand over a worn side table, she smiled. "That's good news since keeping it as is would make the whole recluse thing you've got going a cliché and give you a *troll under the bridge* vibe that would be hard to shake."

"I'm not a recluse, Olivia. Just a man who'd like to be left alone."

Ignoring the not-so-subtle hint, she studied the harsh planes of Zane's face and decided his noble forehead, strong Roman nose, and lush mouth made him quite handsome. Too bad he had the personality of a prickly porcupine.

LEA HART

She let out a quiet sigh and guessed the fantasy about them becoming great friends might not be possible after all. "So, tell me, neighbor, what brings you to our little corner of the world? Did you retire from the military and decide the old family homestead was the perfect place to hide out?" Tapping her finger against her lip, she gave him a slow up and down. "Or are you a super-spy that needs to stay below the radar?" She held up her hand. "No, wait, are you a tech genius that needs a dark basement from which to operate?"

Zane leaned against the banister. "You don't get out much, do you?"

"Why would you say that?" she asked with a laugh, doing her best to ignore his arm porn and thickly columned neck.

"Because you talk…a lot." He moved the foil package from one hand to the other. "And ask a lot of personal questions."

She took two steps closer and rested her hand on his massive forearm. "I haven't even gotten started. Before too long, I'll be pulling on all your loose threads and unraveling your story one clue at a time." Expecting the audacious statement to be rebutted, she was surprised when he remained silent.

The air thickened, and she didn't think the Hawker family ghosts were responsible. It tasted a little forbidden, unnamable, and quite unexpected.

A stream of anticipation whipped through her veins, and she knew it was a sign that something was going to happen. Would it be friendship, a truce, or…a thing so delicious it couldn't be spoken about in polite company?

Clearing her throat, she lifted her hand away from his warm skin. "Anyway, to answer your earlier question, I do get out and am related to more than half the town. So, I have loads of people to chat with but have decided we should at least know the basics about one another."

"Why?" he asked, curiosity lacing his voice.

"Because we're the only two out here, and it would be weird if we didn't."

"Agree to disagree," he mumbled as he stepped back.

Olivia took the bread out of his hand and ignored his lack of enthusiasm. "Is the kitchen still in the back of the house, or have you changed the layout?"

"I'm not going to get rid of you anytime soon, am I?"

"No way." She leaned into his massive shoulder and grinned. "The way you're acting tells me this could be my only chance to hang out with your ghosts, so I'd be a fool not to make the most of it."

"You picked up on that, did you?"

"Ha-ha! I'm not obtuse." Stepping away, she turned toward the long hall. "I'm just ignoring your sad attempts to get rid of me."

"I don't think they can be characterized as sad."

"Agree to disagree," she replied as she took another step back. "I know that you're going to avoid me like a bad rash from here on out, so I'm going to get acquainted while I can."

"I'm thinking this one visit will be more than enough to satisfy any curiosity burning in your belly."

She gave him an enigmatic smile. "We'll see."

"Has anyone ever compared you to a dog with a bone?"

"Perhaps, once or twice." She hitched her thumb over her shoulder. "Should I make the coffee, or do you want to?"

"I'll make it," he sighed. "Follow me, and let's get this neighbor thing over with."

"Perfect." She trailed behind Zane, admiring his broad back and exceptionally fine behind, knowing the work to break through his walls was going to be worth it. "I just want you to know that when you change your mind and want to become friends, I won't consider it a sign of weakness. In fact, I'll accept all friendly gestures graciously."

"I'll keep that in mind," he called over his shoulder.

Laughing at the disgruntled tone, she walked into the kitchen and let out a happy sigh. "Oh, my, this is kitchen porn in the making." Sliding her hand over the warm wood of the island, she felt a sharp pang of envy. "No wonder your dead relatives want to hang out. This is going to be so, so lovely."

She tore her eyes away from the massive Wolf stove and noticed something flicker in Zane's expression. "Are you okay?"

"Of course," he said gruffly before striding over to a counter on the opposite wall. "I'll just get the coffee started."

"Sounds good. I can't wait to settle in and share all of our dark secrets and hidden desires."

Zane glanced over his shoulder. "Do you believe half the things that come out of your mouth?"

"Yes!"

"An optimist, how..."

"Fantastic," Olivia finished. "I know. Better to believe in miracles than a tragedy is around every corner."

"Not really."

Not able to stop herself, she walked to his side. "Any chance of you changing your mind about that at some point?"

"No. And why would I?"

Lifting her hand, she ran her fingers softly over the road map of scars along his cheek and felt him stiffen beneath her touch. "Because you've already experienced a miracle of epic proportions."

"Or a tragedy that would break most humans," he said quietly.

"You don't look broken," she replied, not able to determine why she'd crossed the invisible line of good manners and touched him so intimately. Sliding her hand away, she let out a quiet breath as pain bloomed in his eyes. "Sometimes…ruin is a gift and a road to transformation. Sometimes it's the precursor to amazing." She let her eyes drop to the floor. "Maybe that's possible for you."

Zane cleared his throat. "Does that amazing include being annoyed by my pushy neighbor and her mongrel dog?"

"Only if you're lucky," she said with a laugh before turning. "Point me to the dishes."

"Top left cupboard, nearest the sink."

"Got it." She smiled and then went to the designated cabinet, knowing she'd meant what she'd said earlier about unraveling his story. Underneath Zane's surly exterior lay a person very much worth knowing.

God willing, he wouldn't make it impossible.

## CHAPTER TWO

Zane descended the staircase and heard a door slam on the third level and tried to guess which of his dead relatives he'd pissed off. There were at least a half-dozen in residence, and he wished he could determine what it would take to get them to move on. "Why didn't you guys put on a show when Olivia was here?"

Hesitating on the landing, he waited to see if they'd bother responding.

Nothing.

Damn spirits never cooperated.

He hit the bottom step and heard a sharp bark. "What the hell?" Stalking toward the front door, he swung it open and saw Bella wagging her tail. "Does the purple ribbon signify your royal lineage?"

Drool dripped from the dog's mouth, and he stepped back when she pushed her way inside. "Seems you take after your mama and don't wait for an invitation." The beast barked in agreement as a cool breeze brushed across his skin, and he knew it was a sign that the family ghosts approved of the intrusion. "In case any of you are interested, this isn't normal."

Again, no response.

"Whatever." He strode down the hall with the dog on his heel and entered the kitchen, trying to remember when speaking to ghosts had become a regular occurrence. It must've happened sometime during his third week in residence.

Giving the room a cursory look, he remembered what Olivia had said about kitchen porn and silently agreed. He'd been outdoing himself with the update and looked forward to making the rest of the house worthy.

Stopping abruptly in the middle of the room, he felt Bella bump into his leg and realized he'd had a positive thought. Weird shit, to be sure, since he couldn't remember the last time he'd looked *forward* to anything.

Certainly, it had to be before he joined the armed services. Happy, woo-woo, mumbo-jumbo wasn't part of life on the front lines as a Green Beret, and he'd never been inclined to move outside his three-foot world to develop the habit.

Was that something he should try and change? Did the new life he was forging have room for some positive vibes?

"Not likely," he murmured as painful memories tore through him, parking themselves in their usual spot against his heart. He'd stood at the side of too many graves in the last several years and struggled almost daily with the reality that he'd survived when so many of his brothers in arms hadn't.

The guilt was crushing on good days and deadly on bad ones. Realizing he was about to be engulfed by a tidal wave of dark thoughts, he let out a long breath. "Don't give in to it." Bella's head pressed against his hand, and he stroked the dog's fur, feeling the bleak emotions recede slightly. He kept himself still and waited until his heartbeat slowed.

"Better," he muttered after several minutes. A doggy smile lit up Bella's unattractive face, and he found himself matching it. "Maybe we should keep that little episode between us." The dog blinked twice, and he let out a short laugh before walking over to the coffee pot. "I hate to admit it, but you're almost as charming as your mama."

He got a happy bark in response as he filled a big mug with coffee and thought about the two-hour visit he'd had with his neighbor. Surprisingly, it hadn't been awful, and if he was honest…wouldn't hate it if it happened again.

Could he chalk it up to how damn beautiful the woman was?

Possibly.

Sure as hell wasn't a man alive who wouldn't want to look at her heart-shaped face with full lips and laughing eyes.

Not that he was going to do anything about being in her company anytime soon. No way.

The last thing he needed was to get involved with someone like Olivia. The care and feeding of a woman like that would require a lot more free time than he was currently in possession of.

Not to mention the mental health and emotional intelligence it would require.

He didn't have much of either, and the short amount of time they'd spent together told him that would never suffice. And since he never entered a battle space he couldn't dominate, he was going to keep his distance.

Right after he returned her dog.

Zane walked toward the two-story house that was a mile from his and let out a low whistle when he got close. He'd seen it from the road they shared more times than he could count but never taken the time to study it.

The home was painted dark green and reminded him of a glammed-up summer cabin. There was a small enclosed front porch draped in ivy and an American flag waving in the breeze. The only thing that seemed out of place was the abandoned Ferris wheel that dominated the empty field to the left of the house.

There had to be an interesting story there.

He gulped his coffee and watched Bella run toward the back of the house with a happy bark. "Delivered, safe and sound," he mumbled before taking another look around. He didn't catch sight of Oliva and decided to get away while he could.

It's not like he had the time or inclination for another long conversation.

And seeing her heart-stopping smile wouldn't change his day in any way.

Spinning around, he took a step and heard the slap of a screen door. "So close," he muttered right before he heard the pretty lilt of his neighbor's voice.

"Did you stop by for more banana bread?"

He turned slowly and was glad that he'd worn his dark aviator sunglasses since it allowed him to enjoy the visual feast her curves and dips provided.

Making sure he gave away nothing, he tilted his head. "Your dog showed up at my door, and I brought her back."

"How sweet," Olivia said as she stepped down the short staircase.

"Not particularly." Keeping his expression neutral, he watched her move into his personal space. "Don't want to add dog-napper to my list of sins."

"How long of a list of sins do you possess?" she asked, looking up. "And will you tell me the juicy ones?"

"No," he sputtered, trying to ignore the mischievousness in her gaze.

She clasped her hands behind her back and sighed. "Fine, tell me the boring ones."

"That would be a hard no."

"You're no fun." She frowned and stalked off to a metal table next to the porch and picked up a bowl. "But I forgive you since you brought Bella home."

"So relieved." He followed her and watched her scoop a handful of nuggets out of the metal container, creating a heart on the table. "What in the world are you doing?"

"Luring the big black cat from the woods closer."

"With a heart?"

She gave him a slow once over. "Yes, I want him to know that he's welcome."

"Interesting."

"I'm just trying to keep up the family tradition."

"Which is?"

"My forbearers settled the town and named it Haven in hopes that misfits, oddballs, loners, and rebels would feel welcome."

He lifted out a handful of food and filled in the bottom of the heart. "Guess that explains why mine decided to call this place home since they've all had their eccentricities."

"I love a good peculiarity and am proud to be a part of our population of twenty-five thousand free-thinking souls." She bumped his shoulder. "Truth be told, it helps me maintain the illusion that I'm not all that quirky."

"Solid strategy," he murmured, not understanding the sudden need to shift closer. Placing an iron fist of control around the impulse to run his finger over the soft skin of her neck, he ignored the ripple of awareness.

Mate, claim, and devour were the words skidding across his mind, and he couldn't understand why Olivia was the one igniting the long-forgotten need for human connection.

The sound of a car engine sounded in the distance, and he let out a breath, welcoming the interruption. "Expecting someone?"

"My sister," Olivia replied, brushing off her hands. "Which means luck is on your side, and you get to meet the prettiest of the Bennett sisters."

*I already have*, he thought as Olivia took two steps.

She held out her hand. "Come and meet her."

"Another time." He headed toward the path that led to his house. "Yesterday filled my quota for human interaction for the week."

"Alright, but feel free to stop by anytime."

He gave her a salute and then strode down the rutted road. Waiting for the familiar feeling of relief to bloom, he was surprised when a stab of regret showed up instead.

Telling himself it had nothing to do with his pretty neighbor and her quirks, he quickened his pace, vowing to stay away from temptation.

If something like that was even possible.

***

Watching her neighbor stalk away, Olivia let out a sigh and decided the short encounter didn't do anything to move their friendship forward. But it didn't do anything to decimate the small start they'd made, either.

Bella bounded forward, and she opened her arms, welcoming her dog with kisses. "Good job, girl; you did exactly what we discussed and made that big, beautiful man step outside his routine."

"Who's routine?" Lucy called out as she picked her way across the mud puddles.

"My neighbors'," Olivia answered, admiring her auburn-haired sister's show girl body encased in a flattering dress. "Love the look, Lucy. That day dress is doing all kinds of sinful things for your figure."

"Good," she said flatly. "Because I want that snake of a man who I used to date to feel overwhelming regret every time he catches a glimpse of me."

Olivia took her older sister's hand. "Are you and Ken on the outs again?"

"We're done," Lucy replied firmly. "Never to be resurrected. Finito!"

"Do you want to talk about it?"

"Good Lord, no." Leaning back, she waggled her finger in the direction of Zane's retreating form. "I'd much rather discuss your hot neighbor."

"We'll need chocolate muffins to go with that convo, so come inside."

"Oohhhh," Lucy said, "that's exciting and makes me think the tea you're about to spill is going to be hot."

"Unfortunately, it's lukewarm at best."

"That's a shame," she replied quietly, "since I was planning on living through you vicariously for the foreseeable future."

"I doubt that will be necessary since the men of this town will be buzzing around you like bees the minute your breakup becomes public knowledge."

"I hope not. I've known most of them since Kindergarten and remember vividly when they ate their boogers." She made a frown. "There's not one decent prospect in all of Haven, and I might have to follow our baby sister's footsteps and move out of town to find a man worth holding onto."

"Callie didn't move up North for love; she went to pursue her career."

"And happened to find a fab man along the way."

"True. But I doubt the ties that have kept us bound to this town will loosen anytime soon."

Lucy let out a dramatic sigh. "I know, but every once in a while, I like to pretend it's possible."

Olivia tugged her sister's hand toward the front door. "Let's go fix our lackluster love lives with chocolate."

"Might as well."

As she and her sister tromped into the house, Olivia thought about the man at the end of Lady Bug lane and wondered if he'd ever find her...not annoying.

Once she and her sister were comfortably settled on the enclosed back porch, Olivia gave Lucy an assessing gaze. "Is it over-over with Ken, or have you two just had another knockdown war of words that will take a couple of days to get over?"

"There is no coming back from the things he said. I can happily report that I've seen the light and have set fire to the bridge that once connected us."

"So, you've decided to go with the nuclear option then?"

"Absolutely, and I look forward to the peaceful days ahead," Lucy replied. "No more drama for this llama."

Cutting her muffin in half, she prayed her sister was truly over the town's golden boy. They'd never been much of a match, and she always suspected that underneath Ken's perfect façade lay a heart filled with darkness. Or some fairly bad intentions. Either way, her sister deserved more. She lifted a piece of her muffin and tapped it against her Lucy's. "Cheers, to new beginnings."

"Indeed."

"Hey, before I forget, is our book club meeting still on for Thursday?"

"Yes," Lucy said after taking a sip of her coffee. "I'll send out a reminder tomorrow because no one is going to want to miss the question and answer Skype session I've got scheduled with the author."

"I can't believe you got Ariella Buckwitz to agree to speak with our little group. She's a rock star of regency romance, and I hope she's as funny in person as she is on the page." She stirred another heaping teaspoon of sugar into her coffee. "I'm gaga over the woman."

"Who isn't?" Lucy replied. "My little bookstore may be small in size, but it's enormous in influence, and Ariella is appreciative of all the online pimping I've done for her fabulous books."

"Is Grams going to be joining us?"

"Assuming you're asking that rhetorically since our gin-swilling, caftan wearing, bon-vivant of a grandmother would never miss a get together where drinks and nibbles are present."

"Just wanted to make sure," Olivia said before she took a bite of her yummy muffin. She let the dark chocolate chunks melt against her tongue and felt Bella's head on her knee. "We both know that chocolate isn't good for you." Her dog slid her face away and let out a little whimper before collapsing on the ground.

"Seems you found a dog that's as dramatic as Grams."

Olivia slid her bare foot along Bella's back. "I think they could give the other a run for their money, that's for sure."

"Tell me about your neighbor; is he too handsome for words?"

"Yes, and no," Olivia replied. "Half his face is littered with red scars, and his neck is mottled with burns, but none of that detracts from his devastating magnetism. It almost makes him a tiny bit more appealing since he'd be too handsome otherwise."

"Really?" Lucy asked. "Guess I have to see him in person to grasp his appeal."

"He's rather unfriendly and gruff when you first speak to him, but after a couple of hours, he warms right up." She watched her sister's signature eye roll and let out a huff. "What…it's true."

"No doubt, but why am I'm getting the feeling that this poor man is going to be subjected to your efforts to save him?"

"He's 6'3", two hundred plus pounds of muscle and determination. He was a Green Beret and could probably take out a man with nothing more than a post-it-note. There is nothing about him that needs saving, and truth be told," she let out a sigh, "it would be me who would benefit from his company."

"Ooohhhh," Lucy replied quietly. "You got the *feeling*, didn't you?"

Picking at the crumbs on her plate, she nodded. "I did, and the closer I got, the more intense it became. It was like that force field Grams is always yammering about. It's not nonsense, Luce, and I'm very confused why God made it possible with a man who's a grump and finds me more than a tad irritating."

"Did you do that thing where you forget about personal space and chatter on about any random thing that comes to your mind?"

"Yes," she whispered. "It was so, so bad."

"Think you'll be able to get ahold of yourself next time you see him?"

Olivia shook her head slowly. "Not a chance in the world. He's a flame that I can't stay away from. I sent my poor Bella over there this morning, so he'd have no choice but to return her. I've stooped quite low and will likely do it again the minute I can come up with a plan."

Lucy patted her sister's hand. "I guess the only thing we can do is embrace it and figure out a way to minimize the fallout."

"Maybe there's some kind of spell I can cast on him, so he doesn't find me so unappealing. Do you have any of those witchcraft books on the sale table anymore?"

"No," Lucy replied sadly. "Betsy Yarlin bought them when I dropped the price to $5.99. Lord knows what she plans on doing with them, but I'd say Hoyt

Doherty is likely the center of whatever she's got in mind."

"Bless her heart," Olivia replied quietly, wishing she'd grabbed a few while she had the chance. Feeling a kinship with the woman who lived across the lake, she wondered if perhaps she'd share the spells that succeeded.

"Don't," Lucy said firmly.

"I wasn't," Olivia replied with an innocent smile. "I'm not dumb enough to interfere with the universe's plan."

"Let's hope so."

Olivia crossed her fingers under the table, knowing she wouldn't interfere, but might help things along should the right opportunity present itself.

## CHAPTER THREE

Zane grabbed his tool bag off the hall table and heard the rumble of an approaching car. "Please don't let it be well-intentioned town folks or anyone from my family." He looked through the small window that flanked the right side of the door and let out a groan when he spied his older brother, Asher, emerging from a car.

"Why do they always send the golden boy?" he groused, swinging open the door. "Guess no one felt like paying attention to my request to be left alone."

"Brother, you know us Hawkers don't leave one another in peace for long. We're genetically predisposed to be in one another's business, no matter the consequence."

Shaking his head at his sibling that resembled a Ralph Lauren model, he told himself that a couple of days of brotherly bonding wouldn't kill him. "Just know that I plan on sending the most troublesome family ghosts your way. So, don't be thinking a decent night's sleep is possible while in residence."

Asher pulled a bag out of the back seat along with a cooler. "We both know there isn't a person alive or dead who can resist my charms for long. I expect to have them wrangled and be sleeping like a baby before the day on the calendar changes."

"Sure, sure," Zane replied as he trundled down the stairs and took the red cooler out of his brother's hands. "Did Mama fill this thing with my favorites, or did you stop at the liquor store on the way in and load up on our favorite beer?"

"Both," Asher replied before slapping Zane on the back. "And for the record, I probably need this visit more than you."

"So, the family rumor mill wasn't inaccurate?"

"Nope!"

"Am I gonna get the full download on your fiery departure from the Navy while you're here?"

"Yep, just get me liquored up, and I'll bore you with every gruesome detail."

Taking a minute to study his brother's perfect features, he noted that beneath his perpetual shit-eating grin lay something sad. A thing he never thought possible for the man who never had a bad day or took a wrong turn. "Well, come inside, and I'll show you the renovations."

"Sounds good."

Before they made it through the front door, Zane heard the now-familiar bark of Bella and glanced over his shoulder. "Guess it's time for her daily visit."

"Who does the mongrel belong to?" Asher asked. "And why does it have a baby blue silk ribbon tied around its collar?"

"Bella is the neighbor's dog, and believe it or not, the woman wears a matching ribbon almost every day."

"You mean the hot dish I saw standing next to the mailbox is your neighbor?"

Frowning, Zane set the cooler down and put out his hands to stop Bella before she skidded into his family jewels. He patted the dog's chest and didn't like the flare of anger his brother's comment produced. "Olivia is not a hot dish. She's a…"

Asher arched his brow. "Note taken and territory successfully marked, brother."

"No, it's not like that. It's just…"

"No need to explain. And for the record, Bravo. It's about damn time you took a step into the land of the living."

Zane picked up the cooler and walked into the house. "There's no step, and I'm not interested in my neighbor. For your information, she's pushy as hell, nosy, and has no respect for personal space."

Asher winked at Bella and then followed the dog into the house. "Methinks he protests too much. What do you say, dog, does Zane have the hots for your mama?"

A loud bark smacked against the walls of the old house, and being the smart man he was, Zane ignored it and headed straight into the kitchen to unpack the food his mother had made.

The moment he stepped inside the room, the large kitchen window rattled in its casing, and he knew one of the family spirits trying to send him a message from the great beyond. "Not interested," he murmured as he slid two six-packs of his favorite brew into the restaurant-grade fridge.

Asher strolled in with Bella on his heel and whistled. "You weren't exaggerating when you said the kitchen was going to make professional chefs weep."

Looking up, he smirked. "Considering I never oversell anything, it shouldn't be a surprise."

"Point taken," Asher said, leaning against the island. "Should we return the dog before we start in on the beer or call fancy pants from down the lane to come and retrieve her beast of burden?"

"I'll take the dog back, and you can get settled."

"No way, man. I'm not gonna miss out on meeting my brother's crush."

"You remember that I'm the one in possession of all the deadly skills, right?"

"All the Hawker men are lethal," Asher replied. "Shove that food in the fridge, and let's go visitin'."

Deciding that any reaction was a bad one, Zane took a couple of long breaths and told himself that Olivia meeting his handsome as hell brother wasn't going to be a big deal.

Zane looked up at the sky and noted a distinct lack of storm clouds or anything else that would explain the strange and curious situation. Perhaps it just needed another minute.

He waited quietly and couldn't understand why Olivia didn't flutter her eyes and start talking a hundred miles a minute in Asher's presence. Perhaps she was coming down with something.

What other explanation could there be for her polite smile?

It simply didn't make any sense. She'd been a chatterbox every time they'd been together and standing as close to him as a lover. Why wasn't she doing the same with his brother? "You feeling okay?"

Olivia straightened Bella's bow and then did the same to her own. "Of course, why wouldn't I be?"

"No reason," he replied quietly.

"Are *you* okay?" she asked as she lifted her hand to his forehead. "Half the town has come down with the flu." Lifting her eyes, she stroked his skin gently. "You don't feel hot, and since you don't mix with the locals, it would be all but impossible for you to catch the latest bug."

Ignoring the pleasure her cool hand produced, he cleared his throat. "I never get sick."

"He doesn't," Asher confirmed with laughter in his voice. "But maybe you should see if I'm running a temperature."

Olivia glanced over her shoulder. "You look fine."

Zane took a step back and watched Olivia move closer, making it all but impossible for several of their body parts not to collide.

Maybe the apocalypse had begun without him noticing. What other explanation could there be for her ignoring the man so few could?

"I can make you soup, just in case," Olivia said, taking his hand. "Because getting sick while your brother is here would be such a bummer."

"Not necessary."

"I like soup," Asher called out.

Olivia ignored the comment, and Zane bit back a snicker when he noticed Asher's incredulous expression. He'd never been rejected within the continental United States by any female between the ages of eight of eighty and bearing witness to the first occurrence wasn't…horrible. He squeezed Olivia's hand and then released it. "We're going to head back to the house."

"Okay." She played with the ends of her hair and smiled. "Thanks for returning my sweet dog. I don't know why she's suddenly become besotted with you."

"Me either," Zane replied as he watched her bite her bottom lip. Ignoring the dirty picture that filled his mind, he shook his head and tried to clear the lust that was rolling in like a freight train. "So, we'll be going..."

"Are you sure?"

"Yes...absolutely."

"Because if you two wanted to hang out, I could make sandwiches or something."

Not able to stop himself, he brushed a loose strand of hair away from her cheek. "We've got a ton of food at home."

She let out a sigh. "Alright."

Zane took a reluctant step back, gave Olivia a nod, and ignored the knowing look on his brother's face. "Take care."

"You, too."

Asher stepped around his brother and headed toward the Hawker homestead. "I can't watch this; it's too damn painful."

He watched confusion color Olivia's face. "Ignore him." Spinning around before he made more of an idiot of himself, Zane strode toward his house and vowed to keep his distance.

Again.

\*\*\*

The birds chirped happily in the jacaranda trees that lined Main Street, and Olivia figured they were singing their hearts out because spring had finally arrived and the mating season was in full swing.

Feeling a sense of optimism, she waved to the town mayor and then pushed through the screen door of her mother's health food shop. "Hi, Mom."

"Hello, Livy bear, what brings you to town? I thought you were under a deadline and chained to your studio."

"I am and should be finishing the drawings as we speak."

Elaine moved around a display case that housed essential oils and pressed her hand to Olivia's head. "You look flushed; are you feeling okay?"

"Yes, it's just…my neighbor…"

"Did you finally meet Nan's elusive grandson?"

"I did, indeed." Seeing a hundred questions light up her mother's pretty face, she knew an inquisition was imminent.

"Has the man decided to stay in residence and teach those unhappy spirits who's boss?"

"I think so if the renovation he's started on the kitchen is any indication."

Tipping her daughter's chin up, Elaine clucked her tongue. "Bright eyes, rosy cheeks, and a smile that can't be stopped. Does the recluse at the end of Lady Bug Lane have my daughter smitten?"

"Soooooo smitten, Mom." Swinging her hands from side to side, Olivia let out a little squeak. "There is something about him that has me captivated, and I'm reluctant to admit how much he's dominated my thoughts since Monday."

"Is he charming, intelligent, and bowled over by your beauty and charm?"

"Uuhhh, not really," she replied quietly. "He's going with a growly thing, and probably thinks that I'm annoying and pushy."

"So, not a promising start?" Elaine asked.

"No, but for some reason, it hasn't taken the wind out of my sails."

The screen door creaked open, and Olivia looked across the store and watched the most glamourous woman in the Southeast sweep in. "Hey, Grams."

"Helloooo, my beauties. What have I missed?"

"Just the opening chapter of Livy's love story, Mama. I'm going to make a pot of Oolong tea and want you both to sit at the lunch counter."

Olivia gave her mom a nod and then inhaled her grandmother's Ms. Dior perfume before embracing her gently. "My neighbor has me all agog, and I might be about to make some very foolish decisions."

"I adore foolish decisions, especially when it comes to men."

"I know, Grams. And I'm expecting you to give me some real pearls of wisdom on how to proceed."

Margret lifted her elegant hand and wiggled a finger with a ruby the size of a marble. "The man who gave me this inspired some of my most imprudent choices, and at the ripe old age of eighty-two, I can say without a doubt I regret none of them. The memories are delicious, and the consequences, long forgotten."

"I hope to be half as lucky."

Grams smoothed out her cerulean pantsuit and winked. "Then you're going to have to leave your house and kick up your heels a hell of a lot more. Mischief and mayhem cannot be found out in the sticks."

"Never say never," Olivia replied as they both walked over to the lunch counter and slid into the bright pink leather chairs.

Elaine set down a sunny yellow teapot and then pulled down three blue polka dot teacups. "She's besotted with Nan's grandson, so those old woods might finally see some action."

"Mooooom, you can't say that."

Pursing her lips, Elaine poured the tea. "Why, because I'm a widow who hasn't dated much?"

"No! I just don't want to think about my mom, thinking about me…getting action."

"Nonsense," Grams said firmly. "Now, tell us about this boy."

"He's not a boy; he a grown sexy beast of a man," Olivia replied. "He's in his thirties and was a Green Beret. He's built like a bull and has this thing that makes my insides go all jiggly."

"Does he have a kind face?" Elaine asked.

"I think he's handsome, but the scars that litter the right side of his face make him look foreboding, not gentle."

"A warrior," Grams said quietly. "Now, that's something we can work with."

"I'm not sure about that, Mama. Livy just told me he's not interested and finds her exuberant personality a bit challenging."

"In real talk, that means he couldn't find me less appealing," Olivia added before pouring two teaspoons of sugar into her cup and stirring slowly. "Though he didn't seem as repelled when he stopped by earlier with his brother."

"No man could ever be *repelled* by you or your sisters. You three are the loveliest, funniest, smartest, most charming women east of the Mississippi." She squeezed Olivia's cheek.

"I couldn't agree more," Elaine added. "In fact…"

"Stop, you two. We have to face facts and accept that this crush might very well have unrequited tragedy written all over it."

"You've had a full helping of misfortune already," Elaine said after setting down her cup. "This is nothing but a bumpy beginning."

"Here's to hoping," Olivia replied.

Grams looked over the rim of her cup. "And if that doesn't work, we'll simply will it into existence."

Before she could pretend like she was shocked by the statement, a group of women walked into the store, and she watched her mother push away from the counter.

"We'll discuss this more in-depth later," Elaine remarked.

Olivia blew a kiss to her mother and then turned back to her grandmother. "What's with the beady-eyed stare?"

"I want to meet this man and take his measure."

"That might require an act of God since he seems dead set on the whole hermit thing. It's not like you can accidentally-on-purpose run into him in town."

"Dee, over at the post office, said that he gets packages several times a week; doesn't he have to come in to pick them up?"

"I have no idea, but as the town spy and head gossip, you should have the info at your fingertips."

"I'm not a gossip. I merely pass on information that people willingly share with me so that other people can make wise decisions."

"Way to reframe it, Grams."

"Thanks, honey. I've been honing the skill for years."

"Anyway, the chance encounter with Zane will not likely happen anytime soon."

"Guess we'll have to wait and see."

Seeing the glimmer of a devious plan forming in her grandmother's eye was never comfortable, but since it might net some valuable information, Olivia welcomed it.

After all, a girl had to do what she had to do when it came to affairs of the heart, right?

## CHAPTER FOUR

"What in the world is she doing?" Zane asked as he turned down the road he shared with Olivia.

"Looks like she's hacking away at the ivy surrounding the Ferris wheel," Asher replied, leaning forward. "And doing a piss poor job of it."

"We're going to have to stop, aren't we?"

"Only if you don't want to make a trip to the emergency room this afternoon."

"Yeah, the weed whacker looks like it's got the upper hand." Letting out a frustrated groan, Zane pulled in. "You ever feel like the world is pushing in the opposite direction of where you want to go?"

Asher let out a snort and then levered himself out of the truck. "All the time, man."

"Think we should start paying attention to it or just keep a death grip on our illusion of control?"

"I blew my professional life to smithereens, so a new approach may not be a bad idea."

Zane climbed out of the truck, hitched his jeans up, and studied Olivia, knowing that letting go of his idea of how things were going to play out might be best.

Especially since the sight of her in jean shorts was messing with his ability to hold onto a rational thought.

"I can't wait to hear the story behind the Ferris wheel," Asher commented as he smoothed out his T-shirt and then ran his hand through his hair.

"You know she's not interested, right?"

"Of course, but maybe she's got a friend or sister that might think I'm the answer."

"To what?" Zane asked as he headed toward Olivia and the out-of-control garden tool

"Whatever they need."

"You have bought into your own legend, haven't you?" Zane asked.

Taking two long strides, Asher caught up. "Not really, but as an older brother, I'm duty-bound to blow as much smoke as I can."

"If you say so." Calling out Olivia's name loudly, he got no response, so he moved in and hoped she didn't lose her grip on the machine of death. "Olivia!" He watched her gaze slide up and then waved. "Whatcha doing?"

"What?" she shouted back.

He reached over, flipped the switch, and the whining sound cut off abruptly. "Did the plant do something to you?"

"No, why?"

"You're attacking it like it did."

"Maybe she's trying to free the Ferris wheel," Asher commented.

"That's exactly what I'm doing!" Olivia pushed her sunglasses on top of her head. "I took a break from drawing and decided to come out here and…"

"Attack the ivy," Zane finished. "What were you drawing?"

"I'm a medical illustrator and am in the middle of a project for a client. I'm knee-deep in illustrations of atrial septal defects in newborn hearts, and I have to get up every couple of hours and stretch my back."

"No way," Asher commented. "That's so cool."

Zane rolled his eyes at his brother's attempt to ingratiate himself and then turned back to Olivia. "How did you get into that line of work?"

Stepping closer, Olivia blinked several times. "Oh, my goodness, Zane, that's the second question you've asked me today. You better be careful because I may get the idea that you want to become friends."

Deciding her lack of respect for personal boundaries wasn't all that annoying, he looked down and licked his bottom lip as one small bead of sweat rolled slowly from her neck to her collar bone and then blessedly down the sweet valley of her cleavage.

Had there ever been a more erotic sight?

He didn't think so.

Tipping his head, he watched it disappear into the shadows of her shirt and swallowed loudly.

"You okay there, bro?"

"He's fine," Olivia answered quietly, moving closer.

"What?" Zane barked with a rough voice.

Resting her hand lightly on his forearm, Olivia smiled. "You wanted to know about my career."

He realized his brain was nothing more than a plate of scrambled eggs and decided the blame should sit squarely on Olivia's shoulders. How dare she be so…irresistible, smart, and weirdly entertaining. There wasn't a defense for something like that, even for a man who had zero interest in human connection, friendship, and if the pictures filling his mind were true: filthy, soul-satisfying sex.

Good God, what the hell was happening? Sucking in a long breath, he told himself to get it together. "So…drawing…"

"Yes, I've always loved it and decided that creating visual imagery to help advance medical science's knowledge wasn't a bad way to spend my day."

"That's impressive," Zane said, using every ounce of discipline not to let his eyes fall away from her face. No need to make a bad situation worse. He may be physically falling head over heels for the woman, but that didn't mean he should get involved. Mental health was a necessary ingredient in any successful pairing, and he didn't have enough of it to give in to whatever was simmering.

Taking another step closer, Olivia looked up. "I'm more than a crazy lady to attacks wild bushes on random Thursday afternoons."

"Never thought otherwise," he replied, inhaling the scent of her lemon shampoo. "I've also pegged you as the nosy neighbor who makes the best chocolate banana bread in the…"

"World," Olivia finished.

"Yes," he replied, studying the moisture decorating her collar bone. "And…"

"So, about this abandoned amusement park ride, what's the story?" Asher asked.

Swallowing, Zane stepped back and knew the interruption was for the best. Logic and good decisions were nowhere to be found, and the beast within was minutes away from winning.

"It came with the house," Olivia answered. "The previous owners ran one of those small circuses that traveled from town to town and kept this one thing as a memento."

"Why didn't you have it hauled away?" Zane replied as he looked up at the enormous structure.

"Because I thought it would be fun to see if it could be brought back to life. I've always been partial to things that have been discarded and…"

"You thought refurbishing a Ferris wheel would keep you out of trouble?" Asher finished.

"Something like that." Olivia leaned into Zane. "It's possible, don't you think?"

"Not sure," he said, looking the structure over. "Depends on what kind of shape the engine is in."

"If anyone can bring it back to working order, it's you, brother."

"Really?" Olivia asked. "Are you some kind of mechanical genius?"

"Sort of," Asher said as he lifted away a pile of ivy. "He repairs antique clocks and is a savant when it comes to anything with moving parts. He used to take apart the appliances in the house when we were kids and then put them back together. Drove our parents nuts until they noticed that he always made some small improvement that made them work better."

"That's an exaggeration," Zane said firmly.

"It's not, and you should try and get this ride going."

"Would you consider it?" Olivia asked. "Because I would be more than willing to pay for your time." Grabbing his hand, she let out a small squeal. "And love you forever."

"He'll do it for free," Asher said firmly. "We'll come by tomorrow and get rid of the ivy, and then Zane can see what's what."

Not sure how to get out of the gig or if he wanted to, he let out a huff. "I can look, but I make no promises."

"I'd so appreciate it," Olivia added. "And, please, don't feel any pressure to make one of my long-held dreams possible. Because finding another reason to live will certainly happen…at some point." She linked their fingers and looked up. "In the distant future."

Not able to resist the woman's theatrics, Zane let out a rusty chuckle. "You oversold it at the end."

Olivia swung their hands back and forth. "Thought I might've but was on a roll and couldn't stop."

"Guessing that happens more often than not."

"Not really."

Feeling the warm spring air press them closer, Zane closed his eyes and accepted that refusing the woman simply wasn't possible. Nor was killing the growing attraction that he couldn't seem to control.

What that would eventually mean was hard to predict.

\*\*\*

Olivia leaned away from her drawing table and rolled her shoulders, hearing the slam of a car door. "Who could that be?" Bella's excited bark suggested it was someone they knew, so she leaned out her studio window and watched Zane get out of his truck. "Did you miss me already?"

Looking up, he slid his hands on his hips. "I decided to bring some tools over, so we wouldn't have to do it in the morning."

"I'll help." Stepping back from the window, she heard the first words of what sounded like a protest and decided ignoring it was best. He was fighting the small embers of attraction sparking between them, and she didn't want to make it any easier than necessary.

Even though she was fairly confident that he was closed for business.

His emotional doors were nailed shut, and so were the ones guarding his heart. Whatever happened to him on the other side of the world was affecting him to this day, and she didn't think an easy solution would magically materialize.

Sighing, she knew her folly might result in nothing more than a pile of shards from her broken heart, but darn if she could stop herself. "Full steam ahead," she muttered as she checked her reflection in the mirror. She grimaced and wished that she'd taken the time to shower after her tango with the ivy. She smoothed back her ponytail and hoped that Zane wouldn't find her too unpleasant.

She skipped down the staircase quickly and pushed through the front screen door, sucking in a breath when she saw his T-shirt stretch across his shoulders. Lord have mercy, the man was delicious. "How can I help?" she called out.

"Stay out of the way," he yelled back as he lifted a chainsaw out of the truck.

"I'm a lot stronger than I look." Sauntering over, she lifted herself on her tippy toes and studied the various tools. "My goodness, are you going to build me another house?"

"No, I just don't want to be running back and forth tomorrow."

Feeling a moment of regret for roping him into her project, she studied the grim smile decorating his face and knew letting him off the hook was the only answer. "Zane, let's just forget this little undertaking. You're in the middle of redoing your house and taming the ghosts and…whatever else a hermit does. My project is meant to waste my time, not yours."

"What about your earlier comment regarding long-held dreams and me crushing them?"

"I didn't say anything about crushing, did I?"

He set down an enormous clipper. "I'm paraphrasing, so don't choose this moment to become literal and bust my chops."

"That's just it," she said as she moved to his side. "I'm having a horrible attack of guilt and feel bad for jumping on your brother's offer. It was selfish on my part, and…"

"I'm a big boy, Olivia, and wouldn't be doing this unless I wanted to."

"That you are," she said under her breath. Putting her hand on his, she looked down and noticed his fingers were twice as long and decorated in scars where hers were covered in rings. "I'm sure you have a hundred things you'd rather be doing, and I don't want to hold up your renovation."

"I'm waiting on the kitchen counter tops, so I've got a few days free." Zane flipped his hand and wrapped his fingers around her palm. "And…"

"Yes?" she whispered, looking up. The way his green eyes darkened made her heart skitter, and she hoped that it was desire, not annoyance making his breath quicken.

"I decided that I wouldn't mind taking you on…I mean your Ferris wheel and seeing if I can get it running."

Nodding her head slowly, she said a silent hallelujah and decided that making a big deal of what she prayed was a Freudian slip would be foolish. "Okay. If you're in it for the challenge, then that makes sense. As long as you weren't shanghaied into something you've got zero interest in."

"One thing you'll soon learn about me is that I'm unshanghaiable."

"And the zero-interest component?" Holding her breath, she felt his fingers tighten and his body shift closer.

"Definitely not zero."

Letting out a nervous laugh, she pushed herself back on her heels. "Guessing you're not going to give me a number."

"Not a numbers guy, Olivia."

"Fair enough." She slid her hand away and stepped back. "Let me help you unload the rest of this, and then I can give you the info I dug up on Google about this beast of burden."

Zane handed her a roll of black trash bags and grinned. "You can take this."

She lifted her arm and fisted her hand, making the muscle in her arm pop. "I may be small, but I'm no wimp. I lift weights at least twice a month."

Zane circled her bicep with one hand. "Impressive."

"A gentleman wouldn't mock me."

"What gave you the impression that's what I was?"

"Not a thing," she said quietly, picturing several ungentlemanly things he could do to her. Just as she was about to respond, a loud crash occurred near the house. Turning, she saw a streak of black as the cat she'd been feeding was being chased by Bella. She slipped her arm away from Zane's grip and whistled. "Bella, remember what we said about chasing boys who aren't interested."

Bella being the strong-willed woman that she was, ignored the second whistle and tore into the trees after the object of her affection, and Olivia wondered if she wasn't much different. Hadn't she been doing pretty much the same thing with Zane?

Not liking the voice in her head that answered a quick, *hell yeah*, she turned back and vowed to get herself under control.

Or, at the very least, try to be a little more low-key.

## CHAPTER FIVE

The next afternoon, Zane sat in front of the engine that ran the old Ferris wheel and knew that making Olivia's dream come true wasn't going to be easy. He wiped the sweat off his face, studied the gears, and decided the only answer was to take the whole thing apart and start from scratch.

Hearing the slap of a screen door, he looked up and admired his neighbor's legs as she headed in his direction. And immediately told himself a couple of lies about her not being the most tantalizing woman he'd ever encountered.

When none of them stuck, he let out a breath and reluctantly accepted there wasn't a part of her that he didn't want to run his mouth over or a crevice he didn't want to explore. Olivia Bennett was nothing less than the Devil's own candy, and his ability to resist her was diminishing with every minute he spent in her company.

Was it because she was an open book and let every thought spill from her pretty lips without reservation?

Probably.

He'd long been a fan of people who spoke their truth and couldn't help but appreciate that if a thought missed her mouth, then it made it to her face. All he had to do was pay attention to the tilt of her lips, the width of her eyes, and the very unladylike snort she let out whenever she disagreed with something.

The word charming was quickly replacing annoying, and if he weren't careful, she would have him spun up in her web of magic, and he'd never be free.

Which was a hell of a problem since the last thing he needed was to entertain thoughts of him and Olivia becoming something. He wasn't ready to take a woman like that on and knew half-assing it would never be tolerated. Nor would faking it until he made it. She was the real deal, and pretending otherwise would only result in the inevitable knife being plunged into his heart.

"Where's Asher?" Olivia called out as she got closer. "I made him a sandwich."

Pulling himself out of his dark thoughts, he cleared his throat. "He had to go back to the house for a conference call."

"That sounds ominous."

"Not really, he's just trying to decide what his next career move is going to be."

Olivia set down the basket and then unzipped her sweatshirt and tied it around her waist. "Any chance of me hearing why he left JAG?"

"Possible. If you bribe him with food and alcohol, you'll have a halfway decent chance of getting him to spill."

Olivia rubbed her hands together and grinned. "Thanks for the intel; I'll be sure to use it for only nefarious purposes."

"You should have some shame, woman, and pretend like you have only honorable intentions."

"Sorry, no can do." She closed one eye in a wink and then snorted. "No one would believe me if I tried, so it's not worth the bother."

He shook his head as she collapsed near him and watched her pull a towel off the contents of the basket. "What have you got there?"

"Lunch." She pulled out two wet wipes and handed them over. "And what exactly will make you spill your secret desires and dreams? Food, booze, sexual favors? Tell me, so I know how what kind of strategy I need to craft."

He blew out a raspberry and wiped his hands. "And what would you do with that kind of info?"

"Nothing too horrible."

He raised an eyebrow. "Don't hold back now, woman."

"I'm not…"

"Your mouth twisting into a smile is not selling your innocence."

"Fine." She closed the plastic bag and looked up. "I might… use the information when and *if* I came up with a spell."

"A what?"

"Nothing." She dropped her eyes and dug into the basket. "Never mind, forget I ever mentioned it."

"There's no way I can *never mind* the word spell." Seeing her fingers twist together let him know she was nervous—a condition he would've sworn she was immune to.

Olivia let out a gust of air. "If you must know, it would be more of a plan of seduction than a spell, per se." She flapped her hands in front of her face. "Don't make me say more."

He leaned in, taking her hands. "The truth will set you free."

"I doubt it."

He pressed their joined hands against his chest. "You gotta tell me what you're cooking up in that twisty mind, Liv."

She tilted her head. "But do I, though?"

Sucked into the vortex of her smile, he found himself ready to make a dozen promises he likely wouldn't be able to keep. "About that spell…"

Pulling her hands away, she folded them in her lap. "We both know that I have a crush, so I might've entertained a few ideas of how I could make myself less objectionable…to you."

"You're not objectionable." He snorted. "You're the exact opposite."

"Really?"

"Of course. You're sexy as hell, smart, kind, and…"

"Annoying?"

"A little. But not in a bad way."

Olivia raised an eyebrow. "Because there's a good side to annoying?"

"Apparently," he replied quietly. Leaning back on his hands, he looked across the yard and didn't know what he could say that wouldn't be cheesy. He'd never had a ton of game when it came to women, and now that he was a scarred vet with more than one mental health issue, he had even less.

But he had to come up with something because having an incredible woman confess to a crush was as close as he'd come to a miracle in a long time. "Liv, it's just that…"

"You're not into relationships and don't want to make our neighbor thing awkward by having a delicious, dirty tryst and would just like to be friends?"

Of all the words that came out of her mouth, the only three that stuck were delicious, dirty, and tryst. A hive of killer hornets buzzed in his head, and all he could visualize was he and Liv doing filthy things to one another…again and again. Tryst his ass. He'd need a good long while to slake his need for the woman whose knee was touching his.

"Turkey with brie or roast beef and arugula?"

"What?" he asked as he lifted his eyes and tried to untangle the lustful thoughts twisting his brain into a knot.

Olivia held up two sandwiches. "Which one would you like?"

"Whatever you don't want."

"I like them both, so you choose."

He took the sandwich in her right hand and smiled, knowing that he owed her some kind of response. Leaving her words out there without acknowledgment was cowardly, and that was one thing he wasn't. "Liv, about what you said earlier…"

"Let's just leave it be." She handed him a bottle of iced tea. "Friends. That's what we'll be."

"Okay. That'll probably be best." He popped the top off the cold drink and wished that he were in a better place. Because if he were, there would be no stopping him from sweeping Olivia off her very pretty feet. "You didn't have to make all this food."

"Of course, I did. You and your brother freed the Ferris wheel this morning, and feeding you is the least I can do."

Before he could respond, he heard a phone chirp and watched Olivia slide hers out of the basket and read something with a smile. "Good news?"

"Yes, my sister confirmed that I can bring Bella to book club." Unwrapping her sandwich, she plucked out a piece of brie. "Which, for the record, is very generous, in light of the fact that my sweet dog hasn't had the best manners when we've been to the bookstore."

"Does your sister own the one in town?"

"She sure does and has an impressive online business. A lot of people in the know consider her to be an expert on almost every genre of romance." She popped the cheese into her mouth. "If you ever want a tour of our lovely hamlet, let me know. I'd be happy to introduce you around."

He winced, thinking of all the curious stares he'd have to endure. "I'll keep that in mind."

"Which is man-speak for a big fat no."

"I've only been in residence for two months; it's not like I need to rush into anything."

Olivia narrowed her eyes. "I thought you'd only moved in a month ago; how did you evade my superior spy skills for thirty days?"

"Came in the dead of night with enough supplies to make going to town unnecessary."

"How creepy and disturbing."

"Thanks," Zane replied. "I do what I can." He unwrapped his sandwich, took a big bite, and all but moaned. The roast beef was rare, the arugula spicy, and the generous layer of mayo, perfection. Maybe bringing the Ferris wheel back to life wasn't going to be such a chore after all. "This is damn good."

"Thanks," she replied. "I got the idea from Phyllis. She and her wife, Grace, run the coffee shop in town." She passed over a napkin. "It's just down from my mom's health food store and has a red awning."

"Haven't spent much time on Main Street," Zane commented before wiping his mouth. "The shops look kinda perfect and make me think that I've stumbled on to a movie set."

"Haven certainly has all the charm of town featured in a Hallmark movie."

"A what?"

"Hallmark movies, surely you've heard of them."

"Guess I missed that particular piece of American culture when I was OCONUS for the last several years."

"O-what?"

"Outside Continental United States Overseas."

"Very impressive military speak, Mr. Hawker."

He took a handful of chips out of the bag she offered. "Don't even realize when I'm using it since I grew up in a Navy family. All four of my brothers and I have served in a branch of the military, and it's no small miracle that we're able to speak civilian at all."

"I'll want the full story of the Hawker family history at some point. My goodness, how did your mom survive five boys?"

"With a will of steel and a healthy sense of humor. May Hawker is a force to be reckoned with and never let any one of us get away with a thing."

"You're kind of your own force, so it makes sense that you've got a genetic marker for it."

Biting back a smile, he concentrated on his sandwich and knew the real force was her. Olivia and a block of C12 had a lot in common, and he would be wise to use the same care with the woman as he would the deadly explosive.

"So, give me the highlights of the Hawker brothers."

"Okay, but I'll give you the abbreviated version." He brushed his hands off. "Rorke is the oldest and is retired from the Teams. He's running the SAI office in Virginia Beach. Asher is next, and, as you've heard, is about to retire from the Navy. Birch is the third in line. He was a PJ for a bunch of years and is now running around the world involved with black ops for an off-the-books agency."

"Wait, what kind of agency?"

"The kind we don't talk about."

"That's disappointing." She leaned in. "I'm an excellent secret keeper, so if you ever…"

"I won't," he finished, telling himself he didn't want to know how her lips tasted. "Anyway, I'm next, and Colt is the baby of the family. He's on the Teams in San Diego and by all accounts having the time of his life."

"Wow, too bad you're all such under-achievers."

"Yeah, we're all waiting for the second act to really do something worthwhile."

"Clearly," she said, covering his hand.

He coughed and then picked up his sandwich. *No big deal.* So what if her touch lit up a part of him he would've sworn was non-existent.

Olivia slipped her hand away and lifted a book out of the basket. "I have one more chapter to read before our book club meeting tonight, so I hope you don't mind if I do that while you fiddle with the…," she waved her finger toward the metal box, "disaster."

"You don't have to keep me company, Liv."

"But I want to. Unless having me nearby will be annoying."

"Not annoying, but certainly distracting."

Olivia swayed back and forth and smiled widely. "Whoop, whoop. I'm wearing you down and think that big-dick energy might soon be set free."

Choking, he sat forward and coughed. Taking a slug of iced tea, he swallowed and was grateful when he could drag in a lungful of air. "What did you say?"

Olivia sat up and patted him on the back. "Not going to repeat it."

Straightening, he took several deep breaths. "Oh, yes, you are. What in the hell is big-dick energy?"

"It's what you've got." She batted her hand around Zane's body. "It's a combination of alpha cool, swagga, and quiet confidence."

"And apparently a big dick."

"That's just a euphemism. It's not literal."

He watched her eyes travel to his hands and then down to his boot-clad feet. When they remained there and her cheeks flushed pink, he rolled his eyes. "Size fourteen, babe."

"Really?"

"Yeah, not a thing to lie about."

"Oh, well, I wasn't…"

He leaned down, so they were looking into one another's eyes. "Anything else you want to ask me before I dive back into this sandwich?"

"Nope." She shook her head vigorously. "Not a thing."

"Good." Not able to hold back the smile that broke across his face, he watched her eyes travel back to his hands and decided that if she was going to be the death of him, it might not be the worst way to go.

Not by a long shot.

# CHAPTER SIX

Hearing more than Zane and Asher's voices, Olivia looked out her kitchen window and let out a laugh when she saw her grandmother and sister give the Hawker men wide smiles. "Pray for mercy, boys; it's going to be a bumpy ride."

She closed the oven door, set the timer on her phone, and stepped out to the porch, wondering if the years the men had spent in the military would be enough. It didn't seem all that likely when she saw Zane run his hands over his short hair and give her Grams a pained smile. "Go easy," she muttered as she moved toward the group.

"Good morning, family. Why didn't you let me know you were stopping by?"

"And give you the chance to give these men a fair warning?" Grams trilled. "Not on your life."

"I tried," Lucy said firmly. "But she told me she wouldn't let me borrow her jewelry anymore if I did."

"Good to know where your priorities lay." She kissed her grandmother and then hugged her sister. "Have you all gone through introductions?"

"Of course," Lucy said with a smirk.

"Should I be worried that you two look like you're about to stir the pot and make some trouble?"

"Women who make trouble are the best kind," Asher commented. "And I, for one, am more than happy to get to know the Bennett women."

"And why's that?" Lucy asked as she gave him a slow once over. "You run out of hearts to break and need some new victims?"

"Baby, I'm betting you have me beat by a wide mile when it comes to the heart-breaking business."

"Two peas in a pod," Grams commented. "It'll never work, and you'll bore one another in a week."

Olivia rolled her eyes and moved to Zane's side. "Well, now that we've got that worked out, would you two like to come in and leave these men in peace?"

"No," Lucy replied. "I want to know who's been feeding this man gossip."

Asher lifted Lucy's hand and grinned wickedly. "I don't need to hear tall tales to know that you've got all the men within a hundred-mile radius at your beck and call."

Leaning into Zane, Olivia watched Asher press a small kiss to her sister's hand and knew her grandmother was right. They were two sides of the same coin and would never work.

"Yeah, yeah," Lucy commented. "I've heard it all before."

"I think you boys should come to the annual Haven Spring Fair in the park tomorrow. It's time to do your part to raise funds for the community center," Grams declared loudly. "Now that you're residents of our fine community, it's only right."

"I'm only visiting," Asher proclaimed before letting Lucy's hand go. "But I can write a check if I have to."

"Didn't Nan leave the home to all the Hawker boys?" Grams asked.

"Yes," Zane confirmed. We all own an equal share."

"Then that settles it," Lucy said firmly. "You two will come tomorrow and help out."

"Again," Asher said, "Can't a check be written?"

"No," Lucy replied with a sly smile. "And come to think of it, you'd be perfect for the kissing booth."

Asher dropped an arm around Lucy's shoulder. "Baby, if you wanted a kiss, all you had to do was ask."

"Eeeeew," Lucy pushed his arm off. "Get over yourself. I've done the pretty-boy thing one too many times. I'm going for substance and shared values on the next round."

"And if that doesn't sound like the most boring thing on the planet, then I don't know what does," Asher murmured in reply.

"He'll do it," Zane stated firmly. "But have some crowd control handy, just in case a feeding frenzy erupts."

"Thanks, brother."

"Consider it payback," Zane answered with a smile. "You're due for some hazardous duty."

Grams clapped her hands. "Excellent, with such a handsome boy, we're sure to meet our fundraising goal for the new playground equipment."

Olivia took Zane's hand and swung it back and forth. "Do you want to do the dunk tank or come and help me with the face painting?"

"Neither."

"Oh, poo, you have to pick one."

"Not a fan of crowds."

"Do the face painting," Lucy advised. "The water in the dunk tank is sketchy after the first ten minutes."

"Perfect, you can be my assistant."

"*Really* not a fan of crowds," Zane reiterated.

"But we'll be together, and I promise to protect you from all the people who are dying to get to know the man who's taming the Hawker ghosts."

"Pretty sure they're still running wild," Asher commented. "If the sound of the creaking floorboards last night was any indication."

"They've had free rein of the house for several years," Lucy said. "So, why would they give up their freedom without a fight?"

"Oooh," Olivia said, clapping her hands. "I should have Bea come out and do a smudge on the house."

Grams nodded, twirling her strand of pearls. "Why not have a séance and see if she can get the spirits to stop by and reveal their plans. Maybe there's some agreement you boys can come to with your dead relatives, so you all can coexist peacefully."

"What the what?" Asher exclaimed. "Smudging, séances, agreements…with dead people. No way."

"Way," Olivia replied firmly. "My best friend Bea is a traiteur in training and comes from a long line of women who have the sight. I bet if you two play your cards right, she'll take the house on and get the energy realigned."

Zane crossed his arms. "I think we'll leave the energy where it is for now."

Olivia shrugged. "Okay, just let me know when you're ready."

"Is this the part where we pretend that's a real possibility?" Asher asked.

"Yes," Olivia said as she watched her grandmother move in and begin what she knew was going to be nothing less than a full interrogation. She glanced up at Zane and saw him frown. "What is it?"

"Liv, I don't think the fair is such a good idea. The kids may be freaked out by my scars."

Uncertainty swam in his deep green eyes, and she pressed her hand to his chest. "The kids are not going to care, and I bet they'll assume you're just some kind of superhero. Which, you kind of are since you've done the thing so few have managed and put yourself in peril so that we at home don't have to."

"I'm no hero, Liv."

"Agree to disagree," she replied. "And for the record, I find you very attractive and don't think the scars detract from your appeal in any way."

"You are some kind of crazy, woman."

"In a good way, right?"

"Yeah, Liv. In a totally good way."

"Excellent." Tuning back into the conversation Asher was having with her family, she felt Zane's energy change and hoped that he'd eventually consider opening himself up just a little bit.

Everyone deserved a little happiness.

Including the beautiful, tortured man standing at her side.

## CHAPTER SEVEN

*So much for living a solitary life,* Zane thought, catching his reflection in the rearview mirror as he pulled into the parking lot of Haven's biggest park. "Don't know if I'm up for this."

"Can't be any harder than being a door knocker on the mean streets of Mosul," Asher replied.

"And that's where you'd be wrong," he said quietly. "People have never been my thing, and the older I get, the truer it becomes."

Asher turned and raised an eyebrow. "Hawker men do not shy away from shit. And that includes a small woman who bears a striking resemblance to Tinkerbell's dark cousin. Olivia looks at you like you hung the moon *and* stars, so dig deep, brother, and pull out that bad-ass Green Beret grit and throw a little her way."

"That doesn't make any sense," he replied with a snort. "This is more of a SITFU situation, and I need to suck it the fuck up."

"Whatever, I speak Navy, not Army."

"I'm not even interested in Olivia, so…"

Asher tilted his head out the truck window and grimaced. "Don't be lying when we're in a parked car. I'd like to have at least a half a chance of escaping before lighting strikes, and God sends down his wrath."

Zane let out a breath. "It hasn't even been a week."

"Meaning?"

"Olivia has been in my life for exactly six days. On the first day of our acquaintance, she got herself invited for a full tour of the house and a two-hour conversation. By the second day, I was returning her dog and coming up with a long list of the things I'd like to do to her if…well, never mind."

"Don't stop, Z. You've got me on tenterhooks."

"You were there on day three and saw how she weaved her magic spell and made herself irresistible. Jeez, it was so obvious with the whole soup offer. Is any man strong enough to resist something like that?"

"Certainly not one who was part of an Army Spec Ops team."

Nodding, he felt a fraction better since his brother clearly understood what he was up against. "By day four, I was agreeing to free her damn Ferris wheel and am now single handidly responsible for making her dreams come true. I mean, the woman has powers that I haven't begun to understand."

"And what happened on day five?"

Feeling sweat trickle down his back, he shook his head. "That was by far the worst." He glanced over. "She told me that she had a crush."

Asher slapped his hand on his thigh and grinned wickedly. "Damn devil woman. Doesn't she have any shame?"

"No! And not an ounce of mercy since what man could resist Olivia Bennett's big chocolate-brown eyes and sinful smile when words like that are flung around?"

"Not someone with any sense."

"Damn straight." He rested his hands on his closely shorn hair and gusted out a breath. "And on day six, she kicked me in the nuts and asked me to help out with the kids."

"You might as well grab a ring, propose, and be done with it."

Zane spun his head around and let out a bark of laughter when he saw his brother's knowing smirk. "I'm serious, man." He waved his hand toward the park filled with rides and booths. "This is my nightmare, and yet, here I am, ready to walk into the damn fire."

"Love ain't easy, man."

"This isn't love; it's insanity."

"Same thing."

"Yeah, I can't argue." He pressed his hands into the seat. "I'm on a damn seesaw and can't predict where my mind is going to be from one minute to the next. One second, I'm confident that I can stay away, and the next, I know it's not possible."

"What's your next move?"

Zane leaned forward and caught sight of Olivia, and felt a tiny explosion in his head. Boom went his heart and every objection he'd crafted over the last couple of days. "Hope I freaking survive whatever happens on day seven."

"If you don't, rest easy and know that I'll bury your corpse with all the respect it deserves."

"Appreciate it, brother. He climbed out of the truck and stalked toward the woman who single-handedly was blowing up his carefully laid plans. Was returning to his hermit life even possible again?

Had someone told Zane he'd have grubby little munchkins sitting on his lap and hanging on his back, he would've laughed in their faces. And yet, that's exactly what was occurring—along with an additional three sitting on his feet. Blowing out an exasperated breath, he glanced at the little boy whose hands were digging into his shoulders and shook his head. "I'm not a jungle gym, Sam. Slide down and get your butt back in line, so you can have your face painted."

"You're not allowed to say butt," Kelsey announced. "Big trouble is coming your way!"

"Doubt it," he muttered as he looked down at the girl with freckles. "And why are you still here?"

Kelsey ran her fingers over the spider decorating half her face and smiled. "Because you're a superhero. I need you to make my brother Norman disappear when he's done with the ring toss."

"Why do you want to get rid of him?" Zane asked as he lifted the girl off his knee and set her on her feet.

"Because he tries to use his kung-fu moves on me."

Before he could respond, Kelsey scrambled back on his knee and smiled. "Liv, you gonna help me out here?"

Lifting her eyes away from the unicorn she was painting on a child's arm, she shook her head. "Nope."

"Want to think about it for more than a second?"

"Not really." She waved her hand at the group of kids surrounding them. "You're in charge of keeping me fed, crowd control, and…"

"Anything else you decide?" he finished with a snort.

"Yes!"

"It's important to keep your woman happy," Sam announced as he leaned against Zane's shoulder. "When my dad doesn't do it right, he has to sleep on the couch with the dog."

Zane watched Olivia fight a smile and knew that if he ever took the woman on for real, she'd light his world up in ways he couldn't imagine. Not that he was considering…it.

Kelsey pushed her small fingers into his side, and he looked down. "Girl, you need to quit poking me."

"Why? It's the only way to keep your attention."

"Have you thought of just saying, Mr. Hawker, I have something to ask you?"

"No."

Telling himself he wasn't entertained, he rolled his hand. "Try it next time."

"You need to get Ms. Olivia a corndog. And a lemonade."

"Might as well get a funnel cake, too," Sam added. "My mom loves them and gets real happy whenever she has one." He wiped his nose on his shirt. "Maybe you should get two, just to be safe."

"You hearing this, Liv?"

"Yes, indeed."

Pinning her with a gaze, he watched an indecent smile form on her full lips as the noise of the fair and the chatter of the children fell away. Within a second, there was nothing but the two of them grinning at one another like complete fools. No demons yelling, no ghosts whispering, no voices telling him that what he wanted wasn't possible. It was just him and Olivia in their own world.

Seconds later, the distant sound of music filtered back into his consciousness, and he realized that he'd become *that* guy.

The one he'd always felt sorry for and silently mocked—the one staring at a woman with at least two dozen kids as witnesses.

"Anything you want to add?"

Olivia dug her teeth into her bottom lip and swirled her paintbrush in a glass of water. "I agree with the premise of a man taking care of his woman…"

"And?"

"A woman should also take care of her man. No one comes before the other."

Nodding, he lifted Kelsey off his knee, peeled Sam off his shoulder, and then stood, holding his hand out. "What do you say to a lunch break?"

"Yes," she said quietly. "A hundred times, yes."

"Okay, munchkins, we're out. Go find some other people to crawl on; we'll be back in an hour." A chorus of moans and groans followed the announcement, and he ignored it as he picked his way through the kids and took Olivia's hand. "Ready?"

"I hope so."

"Me too," he murmured as he led her away from the tent.

\*\*\*

"Can I say *I told you so*?"

"Is there any way to stop you?" Zane asked.

"Not really." Olivia stretched her legs out and rested her head against the bench. "It's taken less than a half a day for the local kids to become your biggest fans, just as I predicted. Add to that the many invitations you received to stop by Jasper's bar for a drink, and I'd say you are one popular man."

Zane ran his hand over the right side of his face. "Liv, it doesn't make any sense. People were intimidated by me before half my face was scarred up, and kids have always given me a wide berth. I'm not a man who people have ever gravitated to. All the attention and offers are making me mighty uncomfortable."

"Because it's new or because you find the world too peopley and prefer solitude?"

"Both," he replied quietly. "The stick up my ass warrior thing usually keeps people at a distance. Have I lost my touch?"

"Possible. But I'm guessing your vibe has changed since retirement. I think you're giving off a *gentler giant* thing, and less *I'll decimate you if you irritate me* thing. And, let's face it, the fact you're hanging out with me gives you all kinds of street cred."

Zane snorted. "No doubt."

Shoving her hand into his side, she gave him a good pinch. "Don't doubt my magic powers."

"Believe me, babe, I never considered it for a minute."

"Can I give you some well-intentioned and completely non-self-serving advice?"

"Sure, if something like that even exists."

"You may want to turn down the sexy loner vibe. Because if you keep it turned to ten, your driveway will be filled with willing women, and you'll have a freezer filled with casseroles."

"What kind of casseroles?" he asked with a laugh.

A knot of possessiveness bloomed in her chest, and she told herself to ignore it. "I'm guessing you can get the answer fairly quickly when you go through the stack of phone numbers shoved into your pocket."

Zane rested his hand along the back of the bench. "I'm detecting a note of jealousy, which makes me think you're feeling some kind of way about the phone numbers I allegedly have."

Moving away, she pursed her lips. "That's ridiculous." Feeling his big hand curl over her shoulder, she glanced over. "You're a free man and can do whatever you want."

Moving close enough so their legs were touching, he tugged her against his side. "The last five minutes is the only time you haven't been well inside my personal space. And that tells me you're not being honest."

She pushed her top lip out, studied the townspeople who filled the park, and didn't know why she was trying to lie. It wasn't like she hadn't already confessed to having a crush. The chance of subterfuge had long disappeared, and she might as well own up to the fact she was in the grips of the green-eyed monster and be done with it. "Zane…"

"Yeah, Liv?"

"I might be the tiniest bit concerned that you're going to find one of the beauties too delicious to resist. I mean…you just started finding me not repellant, and I'd hate to miss the chance of …"

"What, babe? What would you like to have a chance at?"

"Uugghhh, why do I open my mouth?" Moving her leg away, she studied her red Converse. "You don't have to hang out this afternoon. I can handle the kids myself."

"Didn't take you for a wimp, Liv."

"What does that mean?" Pushing his arm off, she stood. "I'm fearless!" She rolled her shoulders.

"Okay, maybe that's too strong a word. I'm…mostly willing to do something about my happiness, no matter what it takes."

"Which, for the record, is sexy as hell." Zane levered himself off the bench and took Olivia's hands. "And admirable."

"Really?"

"Yeah."

Feeling her shoulders stiffen, she dropped her head. "Maybe we should sit. I can't keep looking up at you and not end up with a crick in my neck."

"Of course." He collapsed on the bench. "Guess the foot of difference in our heights kind of makes that inevitable."

Olivia sat and crossed her legs. "There isn't a whole foot."

"I'm six foot three, and I'm guessing you come in at right around 5'3."

"I beg your pardon; I'm five foot four and one quarter."

"Good to know."

"What were we talking about?"

Zane lifted his sunglasses off and tucked them into his T-shirt. "You and me."

Looking up, she swallowed. "Now you're giving off that 'big-bad wolf' vibe. Should I be worried?"

"No…"

Pulled into his sea-green eyes, she felt both his enormous hands land gently on her face, cradling her with more care than she thought possible. Leaning into the moment before his mouth landed on hers, she imprinted the memory, so she'd always have it.

Months from now, she wanted to be able to recall with crystal clarity just how full her heart felt.

Closing her eyes, she inhaled his delicious scent and let the anticipation hanging in the air push them closer.

Zane's mouth brushed hers, and she tasted lemonade as she got a glimpse of what life could be if she could kiss him every day. His short scruff offset his soft lips, and every nerve in her body was yelling: more. Digging her hand into his shirt, she felt the strong beat of his heart and told the butterflies doing the cha-cha in her chest to go for it.

Their mouths fused, and life as she knew it...was gone forever.

Dramatic overstatement?

No doubt.

But anything less would be an insult to the absolute best kiss of her life.

Hearing a deep growl rumble in his chest made her move closer and give every last bit of herself to the mating dance their mouths were performing with ease.

Lips parted. Tongues tangled. Claims made.

The man kissed like he meant it, and it was the most perfect: *hello, that's who you are* kiss, and *yes, I'd like to do it for the rest of day, so I can learn you,* one.

Why, she couldn't say. The mechanics were the same as the ones she'd had with other men, but the effect of Zane's kisses was singular.

Feeling his hands move to her waist, she smiled against his mouth as he pulled her into his lap. She gripped his bulgy muscles and let her tongue glide against his. He met her stroke for stroke, and just before she started rocking against him, she heard the sound of children's laughter.

She opened one eye, saw a group of at least a dozen to their left, and pulled her mouth away from Zane's.

"Babe…"

"Audience," she said with a rough voice.

"So?"

"Under the age of consent."

"I think he got her a funnel cake," Sam announced loudly.

Kelsey snorted. "He got her two."

Olivia bit back a laugh and was about to slide off Zane's lap when she felt his grip tighten on her hip. "Honey, we've put on enough of a show."

"And if you get up, we'll be hitting an R rating."

Looking down, she noticed the hard ridge against his jeans and knew instantly his big dick energy was literal. "Uhhhhh…"

"Looking at it with hungry eyes is not helping."

She cleared her throat, tore her eyes away, and nodded. "Of course."

"There's a bunch of kids who are waiting to get their faces painted," Sam announced. "Are you two done kissing, or what?"

Zane gave the kid a hard look. "Don't mess with another man's game and show a little respect."

Sam stood up straight and gave a salute. "Yes, sir."

"I want all you rugrats to go back to the tent and tell the kids that are waiting that we'll be back in fifteen minutes," Zane said with a firm tone. "Any questions?"

Kelsey raised her hand. "I have one?"

"Go ahead," Olivia said.

"Can I be the flower girl at your wedding?"

Stunned, she blinked twice and leaned into Zane. "Well…"

"Go back to the tent as I asked, and we'll think about it," Zane confirmed.

The pack of kids ran off with Kelsey leading them, and Olivia decided that asking what he meant by, 'we'll think about it,' wasn't wise. Did she want him to be a little serious? Yes…she sure did. But she also recognized how crazy that was since they'd only had a couple of promising conversations. "I'm ready for my funnel cake."

"I bet you are," Zane replied with a laugh as he lifted her off his lap.

She smoothed out her T-shirt and was about to let her eyes drop when she heard a growl. "What?"

"Eyes up, babe. We've got a long afternoon ahead of us."

"For your information…"

"Yeah?"

"Oh, never mind." She spun around and marched toward the row of booths offering food and told herself she had everything under control.

## CHAPTER EIGHT

Zane drove along Main Street and took note that the charming store fronts and friendly townspeople didn't grate against his nerves in quite the same way they had when he'd first arrived.

Was his original plan about to be revised? It seemed plausible now that circumstances appeared to be changing.

And by *circumstances*, he, of course, meant Olivia.

And her extremely dangerous mouth.

After they finished with the fair, they'd barely made it to her front porch before they were acting like they had an hour left on earth and needed to make the most of it.

Did hours of kissing and groping change a person irrevocably?

Was it possible to become besotted in seven days?

An involuntary snort escaped, and he knew asking himself such ludicrous questions was a waste of time if the way his heart was acting indicated anything. Not that he'd let that particular organ have a say in anything.

He flexed his fingers and told himself that what he and Olivia had was just a physical thing. Plain and simple. They were two healthy adults enjoying what the good Lord had put them on the earth to do. Nothing less and nothing more.

Mentally patting himself on the back for the fine explanation, he ignored the voice in his head calling bullshit. Hunkering down behind his well-constructed emotional walls, he pretended that the small connection he was beginning to experience was nothing more than an inconvenience. And something that, if avoided properly, would simply disappear.

No need to make more of it than there was. Tapping his finger against the steering wheel, he pulled into the parking lot of the hardware store and shifted his focus to the never-ending to-do list the family manse produced.

He slid into a parking space and was immediately assaulted with the smell of wet asphalt. The distinctive scent that lingered after rain fell on dry soil shot him back to the moment he'd boarded the plane without the three men he'd been responsible for. The all too familiar slide show of the horrific events that led to the loss of his brothers in arms slid across his mind, making a full breath impossible.

He'd been six feet off his target when the blast of hot air knocked him back with unexpected momentum. It was supposed to be a routine patrol op. But it ended up being one of the worst days of his career. They were in contact within ten minutes and doing what they could to evade the grenade that was thrown into the middle of their fire team. His best friend rushed to meet the deadly explosion rather than avoid it. It was a sacrifice that should have been his. Was he ever going to be free of the guilt for failing to bring his men home?

The pressure in his chest eased after several attempts to drag air into his lungs succeeded. He leaned forward, resting his chin on the steering wheel, and studied the brick wall of the store.

A hard truth slid through his gut, and he knew that if he and Liv were ever going to have a chance, he had to do something about the memories and guilt that ruled his life.

Not that he was giving it any real kind of consideration since a minute ago he'd dismissed the idea completely. But calling the Army shrink he'd spoken to all those months ago might not be the worst idea in the world. Hell, if for no other reason than to get his night terrors under control. Something his dead relatives would be sure to appreciate.

He groaned quietly at the prospect of digging into the cesspool his mind had become and pushed himself out of his truck. Was there another option?

Hearing his name, he glanced up and saw two women waving in his direction. He gave them both a tip of his chin and then hightailed it toward the hardware store. What tear in the space-time continuum caused two attractive ladies to be so friendly? Out of all the Hawker brothers, he'd never been the one to garner the attention of women and didn't think the scars he now bore had changed that. Perhaps they thought he could put a good word in with Asher or something.

He pulled open the wide wooden door of the store and cruised up the main aisle slowly. He studied the selection of drills, knowing a man could never have too many. He picked up one he'd seen online and studied the bit.

"That's one of our most popular," a high-pitched voice informed him. "You want me to show you what it can do?"

Zane looked down and studied a teenager with shocking pink braids and oversized glasses. "Not necessary."

"Is it because I'm a girl and you assume I don't know anything about power tools or because you're just browsing while the family ghosts have a rager?"

"Neither," Zane replied firmly. "And what do you know about the Hawker ghosts anyway?"

"A lot more than you'd probably guess." She pushed her hand out. "I'm Zelda, and this is my family's store."

"Nice to meet you." Zane took the girl's small hand and shook it gently. "Guessing you're operating off town gossip, and anything I have to add will be superfluous."

Zelda pulled a stick of gum out of her overalls and unwrapped it. "I've been known to keep my ear to the ground and have amassed a nice pile of facts. But don't be shy 'cause I could always use more."

Zane set the drill on the shelf and crossed his arms. "Is this a fishing expedition or just a desire to confirm already acquired intel?"

"Both." She pushed the gum into her mouth. "And if you could give me the down-low on the gossip that suggests you and your brother are the hot tickets in town and women far and wide are scheming ways to get an invite to your place, I'd appreciate it."

"Really?"

Zelda nodded and then blew a bubble. "Also, feel free to comment on," she leaned closer, "how you got Olivia to kiss you in front of God and everyone."

Why was the idea of him and Olivia kissing all that alarming? He narrowed his gaze. "Has the beauty and the beast thing put everyone back on their heels?"

"No," Zelda said with a smirk. "Olivia hasn't dated much since the tragedy, and…"

"Wait, what tragedy?"

"Oops, maybe I wasn't supposed to say anything." She took several steps back with her Converse squeaking against the linoleum. "Forget I said anything."

"I'd rather not," he called out to Zelda's retreating figure. He ran his hand over his neck and decided he would have to figure out that piece of Olivia's puzzle soon.

A large man with red hair and a matching beard approached. "Welcome to Haven Hardware."

"Thanks," Zane murmured, accepting the man's outstretched hand.

"I'm Allen, and that was my daughter who just," he lifted his fingers and made quotations, "spilled the beans and now has to regroup."

"Didn't notice any bean spilling."

Allen clapped Zane on the back. "I doubt that's true, but I appreciate you suggesting otherwise. He crossed his arms over his barrel chest. "Did you come in for a new set of wrenches? I figure you need a smaller one since the engine on the Ferris wheel is packed tighter than a can of tuna."

Doing his best to acclimate to the rate at which information flew around the small town, he tried to remember what else was on his list. "I actually could use a smaller set and some…"

"Shims," Allen finished. "That old house you got is about as even as my wife's temper, and I bet those cabinets you just installed have settled a lot more than you were planning on."

Zane snorted. "My God, man, is there anything you don't know?"

"If you asked my beloved bride, she'd give you an earful, but since she's busy at the Paint and Sip, I'll say absolutely not." He hitched his thumb over his shoulder. "Follow me, and I'll grab the stuff you need. I'll also include some caulk since Olivia's windows are about due."

He followed Allen down the center of the store. "Olivia and I are…"

All six feet four inches of the town psychic skidded to a stop and spun around. "Please tell me you're not planning on letting an opportunity with such an incredible woman pass you by."

Staggered that Allen had any sort of opinion about he and Olivia's budding friendship, he tried to come up with a response and found he couldn't. "It's not…"

"As the town's occasional arbiter of love advice, it's my job to gently remind you that being the guy on the train is not a story you want any part of."

"What train?"

Allen lifted his eyes to the ceiling, mumbled something, and then returned his gaze to Zane. "It's not a literal train, but one that represents opportunity."

Not sure whether to be pissed or amused that he appeared to need metaphors, he waited for whatever bit of wisdom the man was about to lay down. "I'm listening."

Allen leaned against a display and cleared his throat. "The man who hesitates loses. The man who finds himself in the company of a beguiling woman and does nothing about it will likely be haunted by that *what if* for longer than anyone would like. Don't be that guy. If you encounter a woman on a train, in the street, or just down the road from your house that makes the word irresistible run round and round in your head, for all that is good and right in the world, do something. Anything. Even if it's only an awkward, fumbling, poorly thought out gesture."

Not wanting to encourage more feedback, he nodded. "I'll keep that in mind."

"Please do, because the last thing this town needs is another sad sop parking his rear on a barstool at Jaspers. We've got plenty of bachelors who weren't able to navigate the road to love and believe me, that isn't a group you want to join."

Before Zane could respond, Allen turned and headed toward the back of the store. "Meet me at the counter, and I'll bring the stuff you need."

"Indeed." He scraped his hand over his head and then walked toward the back counter.

Running the advice over in his mind, he rejected more than half of it. After all, he was a man who'd always acted decisively and without a trace of dithering. If he wanted something, he damn well went out and got it. And as for Olivia, he couldn't escape the woman's presence if he wanted to. She was everywhere.

Which meant that he needed to get his mind right because summoning the effort to avoid her and the crazy chemistry they shared was becoming more difficult by the moment.

A thing that could easily lead to disaster for both of them.

\*\*\*

Olivia leaned against the kitchen counter and watched Zane drop his head against the steering wheel of his truck.

Should she go out and see if he was okay?

Would that be too intrusive if he were in the middle of a major freak out?

Feeling Bella lean in, she looked down. "We're going to give him a little space. Running out there fluttering and fussing will only make him resist us that much more."

Bella didn't appear convinced, and she knew that it was time to lead by example. How could she command her dog to have restraint if she weren't able to do the same?

Digging her toes into the rag rug under her feet, she watched the man who had parked himself squarely in the center of her very naughty dreams.

Perhaps he was having some kind of flashback?

Or worse—composing a speech about wanting just to be friends.

Could he be replaying the mind-bending make-out session they'd shared? Because she sure had. Resting her chin on her clasped hands, she closed her eyes, letting every delectable detail play on a loop.

Zane Hawker was a master and more than capable of making lust tear through her limbs like a runaway train. His tight-fisted control had slipped the previous evening, and she knew that if he ever let himself go…he'd be impossible to resist.

Sighing, she thought about the handful of minutes when he'd lost his manners. It had been delicious enough to make her want to quit her hobbies and dedicate all her free time to making it possible again and again.

She bit her bottom lip. "Please don't let him end this thing before we get started." Bella barked in agreement as her cell phone rang. She saw her grandmother's name pop up and slid her finger across the screen. "Grams, I'm very busy staring at the man who has turned my world upside down."

"And how is that working out for you, my darling?"

"About as good as you'd expect."

"Well, don't fret. The way he was looking at you yesterday suggests he's all but enamored with your fine mind, razor-sharp wit, and delicious kindness."

"Half the female population of Haven managed to cram their numbers into his hand yesterday, so his momentary interest might very well have disappeared." She pushed herself away from the window. "He's been sitting in his truck for five minutes with his head against the steering wheel."

"He could be doing some light meditation."

"Zane is like one long exposed nerve, and the chances of him being into breath work is about as likely as me discovering a love of math."

"Maybe he's composing a nice sonnet to seduce you with."

"Are you even trying to make me feel better?" She frowned. "He's probably having an old-fashioned freak-out and coming up with a sad sack of fibs to get rid of me. Men like options, and, as of yesterday, he had a pocketful." A gust of disapproval found its way through the glass of her phone, and she knew Margret wasn't going to let that comment go.

"You are not an option, Olivia Elaine Bennett. And any man who thinks that is not worthy of your time and attention. The only people worth investing in are the ones who see your value and show it in deed and action. If this boy is incapable of seeing that you're a treasure, then he's not the one. Period."

"Zane is not a boy. He's a full-grown man with a chest full of regret, a heart filled with pain, and a mind tortured by memories. I may simply not be his cup of tea."

"And if that's the case, better to know sooner than later."

"Are we sure about that?"

"Yes, my sweet girl."

"That's what I was afraid of." She smoothed out her shirt. "I guess it's time to go out and face the music."

"Indeed."

Seeing the top of Zane's head resting against his steering wheel told her it was likely a tune she wasn't going to care for. "What did you call for, anyway?"

"I want you and your sister to come to lunch tomorrow so we can concoct a plan to get your mama and the sheriff out on a date again."

"Our attempts at playing cupid last year failed miserably. Is it something we should try again?"

"Absolutely. My daughter may have the disposition of a mule, but that doesn't mean we can't overcome it and make a second chance at love possible."

"I suppose the six months that have passed since our last attempt might very well be enough to lull her into a false sense of complacency."

Grams snorted. "Exactly. Be here at twelve, and let's see what kind of devious...I mean effective love trap we can come up with."

"Alright."

"And Olivia..."

"Yes?"

"Don't be afraid to rename the prince in your story. If Zane isn't the one, then another will be along shortly."

"Love you, Grams."

"Love you more."

Olivia slid her finger across the glass and ended the call. "Alright, neighbor, let's see what the next best move is going to be."

Making her way across the gravel driveway, Olivia hoped the conversation she was about to have wasn't going to require a tube of cookie dough and a bottle of wine to get over. When she got close enough to see Zane's pained expression, it was clear that adding a bag of white cheddar Cheetos would not only be prudent but necessary. "Damnit," she muttered quietly. "So much for hot kisses on the porch."

She slowed her pace in an attempt to put off the inevitable *it's not you, it's me speech* and pushed her Keds through the small rocks. "Going to assume the fact that your forehead is scrunched up like a Shar-Pei puppy and your mouth forming a firm line of 'hell no' is not going to bode well for me."

Zane pushed open the door to his truck and dropped his feet to the ground. "Allen said you needed your windows caulked."

"And the news made you sit in your truck for ten minutes in deep meditation?" She eliminated the space that separated them and leaned against the truck door. "I save for my angst for leaky pipes, but that's just me."

"Did you know that everyone in town is talking about us?"

"Not surprising." She rubbed her finger over the edge of the open window. "But considering half of the population spent a month discussing my sister's window display, it's par for the course."

"I'm not the guy on the train, Liv."

Not able to stop herself, she took one of his calloused hands. "Did your trip to the hardware store produce some sort of epiphany?"

Zane slid his hand away and crossed his arms over his chest. "I'm not interested in taking our flirtation further. I can't handle the complications you'd park at my door. I want a peaceful life, and being around you will not make it possible. And…"

"Okay, Zane. I get it. No need to give me the full list of excuses." Surprise and irritation colored his face, and she stepped back. "We'll just exchange the occasional pleasantry. No need for things to get awkward."

"That's it? You're just going to give in and accept it without an argument?"

Not caring for the hard bite of his tone, she crossed her arms. "I'm a civilized person and don't resort to fits when things don't work out my way." Hearing Bella approach, she turned toward her dog and did everything she could to snuff out the famous Bennett temper that was beginning to bloom. The last thing she needed to do was give in to her baser instincts and give Zane the show he was expecting. She may have a crush on the man, but that didn't mean her self-respect had flown the coop. If there wasn't a mutual "hell, yeah" between them, then she wasn't interested.

And yes, she understood how that statement flew in the face of all her previous actions, but there it was. When a man said, no thank you, it was best to take him at his word. She bent down and kissed her dog's head and then threw Zane her best *I don't give a flying fig* smile. "Take care, neighbor."

"You don't want to know why?"

"Not particularly."

Zane pushed himself back in the truck and slammed the door. "Considering you're a person who isn't satisfied until they know every last detail, I find that hard to believe."

Frustration, sadness, and irritation crawled up her spine, and she did everything not to let it show. The last thing she'd give the irksome man was the satisfaction of knowing how deep her disappointment ran. "When a man tells you he's not interested, what more does one need to know?" She narrowed her eyes. "A crush can disappear as quickly as it appears. I appreciate you not stringing me along. I'll simply set my sights elsewhere and find another candidate with whom to share my affection."

"So, your feelings toward me were never that big of a deal?"

"I don't know, Zane; you ripped the opportunity to discover what might be from my hands."

Not wanting to drag out the conversation further, she spun around with her dog at her side and stalked toward her home. Damn man. No doubt he could walk into the most horrific mission without missing a beat. But God forbid he should face his heart.

Silently thanking the wine gods, she was glad she had a cabinet full of therapy.

It was going to take more than a minute to get over the lost opportunity, and she was grateful that she had the means to make it a tad less tragic.

# CHAPTER NINE

Zane watched Asher load his duffle into the car and didn't know what to do with the toxic cocktail of emotions churning in his stomach. If his brother didn't have to put out the flames surrounding his career, he'd ask him to hang around for a couple more weeks.

And not just because putting the family homestead to rights was going to take more than his efforts. He needed his big brother's brutal honesty and sage advice because as much as he hated to admit it, he'd been teetering a lot closer to the edge than normal.

The three days that had passed since terror and old memories bounced off the interior of his truck like a bomb had not been his best.

The demons he kept regular company with had been in overdrive from the moment he'd left the hardware store, and he wished they'd take a freaking break. Not only had they torn at the little confidence he'd cobbled together about him and Olivia, but they'd made too many old failures resurface and gnaw at his bones.

The song and dance was getting old, and he needed to find a way to put the past to rest once and for all. And not just because staying at his end of Lady Bug Lane wasn't going to last for very much longer. Though, that was certainly a big motivator since the muscle in his chest had been relentlessly campaigning for him to hightail it to Olivia's and offer a hundred apologies.

"You done chewing over the biggest mistake of your life?" Asher called out.

"Working on it," he responded before walking down the stairs.

"Despite facts on the ground suggesting otherwise?"

"Yes!" Hearing something knock through the trees, he held his breath in hopes that Bella was about to visit. When the dog didn't appear, he let out a gust of air and knew it was probably best.

Asher pushed his sunglasses down, peering over the top of them. "I kinda want to hand you your ass but know Olivia already did a bang-up job." He thumped the top of his car and then shook his head. "Brother, you somehow managed to trip over a woman who is kind, sexy, and can make you laugh. The only appropriate response to something like that is to wife her up, plant your ass in this small town, and hide her fanny like it's drug money. *Not* torpedo your only chance at happiness.

Zane knew there was something to his brother's skewed advice but didn't think he could put together a time machine fast enough to take advantage of it. "Speaking of nuclear warheads, what are you going to do about the one that imploded your career?"

"I'm gonna wrangle with the powers that be and remind them that if I'm not honorably discharged, I won't hesitate to reveal where the proverbial dead bodies are buried."

"Which answers my question about the veracity of your conviction and the hill you planted your flag on."

"I'm not a pawn that can be used for the Navy's dirty work. The charges that were leveled against the

SEAL were total bullshit *and* politically motivated. I wanted no part of the cake eater's need to cover their asses. Eventually, I'll retire with full honors, start my own firm, and make more bank than I know what to do with."

Zane walked around the car and slapped him on the shoulder. "Proud of you, man."

Pushing his sunglasses up, Asher let out a snort. "It's not like I had a choice."

"Doesn't mean it was easy."

"Hawker men don't do easy."

"Ain't that the truth," Zane said quietly.

"You ever think it's time to do the hard thing and give in to what your heart wants? Fuck your walls, brother; they're not doing you any good. Jump. Because there's no better place for bravery than in love and war. And since you already proved yourself a hundred times on the battlefield, it might be time to have a go at the other."

"Just like that?" Zane asked, knowing the answer.

"Yeah, man. Just like that." Asher gave his brother a brief hug and then climbed into his car. "Rejection lasts a minute, but regret lasts a lifetime."

Not able to deny the truth or the emotion clogging his throat, he stepped back and gave him a tip of his chin. "Till next time."

"Will be sooner than you think."

"Hope so." He watched his brother drive away from the house and knew hermit life no longer held quite the same appeal.

A slice of sun slid through the thick foliage, and he took a step, placing himself in the center of it. The warmth hit his shoulders, and he quietly admitted that he was terrified.

Of letting her go.

*And* letting her in.

Of the day she'd finally open her eyes and see who he was.

Was there an ounce of bravery left in his worn-out soul to see if happiness was still possible?

A brisk breeze skittered across the ground, lifting leaves, and he knew that finding out may not be a choice anymore.

It might be inevitable.

\*\*\*

There was no doubt about it; Olivia resembled a deflated balloon. Her spark had sputtered, her light had dimmed, and eating more Cheetos wasn't going to change a thing. Pushing the half-empty bag to the back of her pantry, she closed the door firmly and decided that getting out of the house was necessary.

A nice hike around the lake would put her to rights. And no doubt, allow her mind to clear long enough so that obliterating the short entanglement with Zane became possible.

Bella bounded into the kitchen, skidded to a stop, and gave her enough of a doggy grin to make some of the battered feelings in her chest slide away. "Let's go feed those awful rosemary crackers to the fish."

Bella tilted her head. "I know that we didn't care for them, but the fish might." She straightened the orange ribbon on her dog's neck, squashed an unbidden picture of Zane's face that tried to float across her mind, and grabbed the bag off the counter. "Fresh air is what we need."

Pushing the screen door open with more force than was necessary, she skipped down the steps with Bella on her heel and heard the rumble of a truck engine. "Please, don't let it be Zane."

Not that she couldn't handle seeing her neighbor because she most certainly could. It's just that she'd prefer not to since he'd made it more than clear that anything beyond the occasional distant wave wouldn't be welcome.

A red truck trundled in her direction, and she smiled when she saw her best friend's face. "Just the visit we need."

Bea pulled in and slung her door open. "I felt your sadness all the way in town and knew I had to come."

"I'm so glad it's you," Olivia exclaimed as she hugged her friend. "I thought another woman was about to deliver a cake or casserole to the Hawker men. There's been a fairly steady parade of them since Monday."

"There's only one Hawker in residence. I saw Asher tear out of town a couple of hours ago."

"Oh," she replied quietly. "Then Zane will just have to deal with the town's beauties on his own."

"The only woman he's interested in is you." Bea took her hand. "His aura is very murky. He doesn't know how to handle his feelings and is engulfed in gray. Poor thing."

"His aura is not my concern. Nor is his chi." She fixed the ribbon in her hair. "Or anything else about his person."

"We both know that's not true." Bea frowned. "The man is working over-time not to fall head over heels in lust. And since we're more evolved, it is our responsibility to extend grace while he goes through the process."

"Is that what you were doing with Asher at the kissing booth?"

"The man certainly doesn't deserve an extra ounce of it," she huffed. "There are few people who cause my good intentions to falter and that...that...infuriating man would test anyone's desire to be a good human!"

Olivia snorted louder than was polite. "Perhaps we should discuss your situation and not mine."

"No, thank you," Bea said firmly. "Since Asher Hawker is of no interest to me." She pushed her fingers into her pocket. "What did Zane say anyway?"

Olivia sniffed. "He told me in no uncertain terms that he had no interest in the chaos I would bring to his life."

"He used the word chaos?"

"I'm almost certain he did." She looked up and then shrugged. "That was the gist, anyway."

Bea rolled her lips together. "That was fear talking. Not his heart."

"Doesn't matter since my crush has evaporated." She snapped her fingers. "Disappeared."

"That kind of nonsense needs a glass of wine."

Olivia whistled for her dog. "We're going for a walk first. I've eaten most of my feelings for the last three days and need to stay away from my pantry for a while."

"Fine." Bea patted Bella's head. "We can discuss your chi on our walk."

"Must we?" Olivia whined as they crossed the road and headed into the woods. "I'm tired of dissecting my dead dreams and unrequited lust."

Bea rolled her eyes. "I see you're honoring Margret and giving into theatrics."

"I don't even know him." She took her best friend's hand. "How did he get ahold of me so quickly? It's not like he's got some great personality and showed me why being friends would in any way not be torture."

"What one's heart desires rarely makes sense."

"My heart never had a chance to get in the game." They tromped through the woods, and she felt some of her more wretched feelings soften. "It was just a stupid crush and likely rooted in nothing more than fantasy."

"If that's true, and I'm not saying it is, then those kinds of feelings can be worked out quickly and dismissed."

"I suppose so," Olivia replied, plucking a flower off a plant. "I haven't enjoyed the company of a man in a while. Maybe I just need some sweaty sex and confused my initial feelings for something more."

"Only one way to find out," Bea said with a knowing smile.

Olivia heard her watch beep with a reminder. "Oh, shoot, I almost forgot; Hoyt is coming over later to see if he can get the Ferris wheel working."

"I bet that'll make Zane crazy. Nothing a man likes less than having someone encroach on their territory."

"Zane doesn't have any territory where I'm concerned," Olivia replied as Bella ran ahead, barking loudly.

"Let me ask you this…"

"Uh-oh, should I be concerned?"

"Of course not." Bea took the mangled flower out of Olivia's hand. "If Zane offered to sex you up with no strings attached, would you accept?"

"I might." She let out a gust of air. "Scratch that. I totally would since it would surely cure me of any lingering fantasies of how we could make one another completely and utterly happy."

Bea grinned. "One good tumble in the sheets could be all you need."

Olivia looked out into the distance. "I can't disagree, despite the fact I've spent the last three days constructing elaborate scenarios in which he suffers greatly." She kicked the ground. "Which just shows that I'm not a good human since he did nothing more than reject me."

"He didn't rebuff *you*. He just couldn't grab hold of his courage to take you on."

Olivia winced. "Knowing that I'm the type of woman that requires more bravery than going into battle is not comforting in any way."

"Getting to the good stuff is never about comfort." Bea put her hand on Liv's shoulder. "But you already knew that."

She ignored the memories that tried to fight their way to the surface. "All this theoretical talk means nothing because Zane is never going to try. Let's be honest; the chance of him pursuing me is about as likely as me deciding that cake is a bad idea."

"Of course."

She narrowed her eyes. "I mean it, Bea. I'm done tripping over myself. The man would have to do something spectacular to get me interested in a sexy shag."

"Not a doubt in my mind."

"Oh, shoot." She caught sight of a large figure in the distance. "Please let it be one of the Doherty brothers." The sound of a happy bark hit her ears, and she had a sinking feeling that the broad back she was looking at was Zane's. "He's going to think I'm tracking him." She scraped her running shoes along the dirt and whistled for her dog.

"Doesn't have to be a thing," Bea said firmly.

"I know, and believe you me; I'm gonna be the coolest cumber you've ever seen." She moved down the trail and saw Zane's face when he turned in her direction.

"Guess God wanted y'all to have a conversation," Bea commented quietly as she followed.

"Can't imagine why." Olivia watched Zane head in their direction and affected a blasé expression. *Not going to say more than necessary!*

"Hello," Zane called out.

Not able to read his tone, she gave him a short wave and then held her hand out for her dog. When Bella bounded over, she let out a quiet sigh. "Let's go, girl." She took Bea's hand and headed toward the upper trail.

"No time to talk, Olivia?"

She turned and scowled. "Didn't think idle chit-chat was your thing?"

"Our conversations were never idle."

"Going forward, they will be." She tilted her head. "You remember my best friend, don't you?"

"Of course." Zane lifted his hand. "Hey, Bea."

"You look well, Zane."

Olivia snorted and watched Zane's mouth form a straight line.

TRUST

"You have something to say, Liv?"

"Nope."

"That's a first."

She did her best to bank her frustration. "Don't worry; I'm not going to fill the air with chatter and throw myself at you anymore."

"About that…"

She dropped her sunglasses. "You've had visitors all week, so I doubt you need any more human contact."

When he didn't make a rebuttal, she pushed her glasses up. "See you around." Not waiting for a response, she headed up the trail and told herself that it wasn't regret coloring Zane's features but relief. From here on out, she planned on giving Zane exactly what he asked for. And if he happened to choke on it…all the better.

## CHAPTER TEN

Zane walked toward his neighbor's porch and told himself there was no way he could eat all the fish he'd caught, and sharing his bounty with Olivia was the right thing to do.

The gesture had everything to do with not being wasteful and nothing to do with how hard his heart had beat the moment they stood close. Hearing what he thought was the low timbre of a man's voice, he quickened his pace and saw Olivia standing next to her Ferris wheel with a man crouched next to the motor box.

"I don't think so," he muttered, moving in the couple's direction. "What kind of person messes with another man's project?"

"If you feel like giving it a shot, Hoyt, then please do."

"No need for that," Zane said sharply.

Olivia whipped her head around. "What in the world are you doing here?"

Zane held up the small cooler in his hand. "I brought you some fish." He stomped over to the ride and dropped it next to his feet. "I'm going to finish the rehab on the engine, Olivia."

"Not necessary." She waved her hand. "Hoyt has volunteered to have a go at it."

The man stood and put his hand out. "We haven't met yet. I'm Hoyt Doherty and run the service station in town."

"Zane Hawker." He took the man's outstretched hand and shook it firmly. "You don't need to dig into the engine. I've got it well in hand."

"Not anymore," Olivia said firmly. "I've decided to hire Hoyt for the job."

Zane watched the man's gaze bounce between the two of them. "I told you that I was happy to take on the project."

"I don't think the word happy was ever used."

Hating that Olivia was treating him like someone she had no interest in, he moved closer. "You told me that I could make your dream come true."

"I'm fairly confident that's not true."

"It sure as hell is, and…"

"I'll head out," Hoyt said quietly. "Seems you two have some stuff to work out."

"We don't have stuff," Olivia replied sharply. "I have my stuff, and Zane has stuff. But we'll never have stuff together."

Hoyt took a few steps back. "Alrighty…just give me a call when you're ready."

"I will," Olivia called out. "Believe me."

"That was ridiculous," Zane said before closing the door on the box that covered the engine. "My stuff, your stuff…jeez."

"Don't you dare mock me." She pinched her mouth together. "Please take your fish and ego home."

"My ego?"

"Yes, your big fat ego that's telling your small male brain that even though you don't want me, no other man can." Lifting her hands, she waved them around. "It's so obvious."

Frustration built in Zane's chest. "If I start a project, then I finish it. Full stop. My…" he pushed his finger toward the decrepit ride, "big or small whatever has nothing to do with it."

"Oh, puleeeze." Fisting her hands, she leaned in. "I don't want you touching my ride."

Zane took a step closer and put his face within a millimeter of hers. "You sure about that?" With his heart beating at the same rate as it did in combat, he found his focus sharpened. Olivia's lemony scent pervaded his nose as the sound of her quickened breaths filled the space between them.

God damn, he wanted her.

"Never been surer of anything in my life," Olivia said breathlessly.

Without thought or consideration for the consequences, he lifted his thumb and ran it slowly over her bottom lip and groaned when her teeth sunk into his soft flesh. "Don't."

"You're not the boss of me."

Confusion and desire stormed through his veins, and he gave in to the feelings he'd been fighting since laying eyes on the damnable woman.

In one motion, he scooped her into his arms and crushed her against his chest as he lay claim to her mouth.

Not sure if she would welcome his crazy gesture, he kept the contact soft but insistent, wishing his will alone could make her like him. Again.

Blessed relief washed across his battered soul when she softened and returned the kiss. Then lust tore through him like a rioting mob, annihilating all the promises he'd made earlier about staying away. Heat slicked his skin, and he swore that the dumb-ass organ in his chest was about to be pushed to its limits.

He kept their mouths touching and spoke against her lips, "I'm sorry. I got spooked and..."

Olivia leaned back and scraped her eyes over his face. "Did you run because you're too stubborn and proud to be bad at something new?"

"What? No!"

Receiving a lifted eyebrow in response, he tightened his hold. "The idea of failing you in any way is too uncomfortable to contemplate. I always succeed. No matter what it takes."

She slid down his chest and let her feet fall to the ground. "Our budding flirtation being the exception."

"I don't like entering a battlespace that can't be dominated."

"The fact that you just compared me to a battlespace tells me that avoiding any," she waved her hand, "entanglement is the smartest choice I could've made."

"I told you that I wasn't any good at this romance stuff." He took her hand and ran a finger over one of the many rings that decorated her long fingers. "I miss your light, Liv."

"Really?"

"So freaking much. I tried to stay away." He took her other hand and felt her stiffen. "Liv…"

"Don't move."

Not caring for the alarm in her voice, he spun around so he could assess the threat. When he spied a fat skunk, he let out a chuckle. "It's just…"

"The most villainous, bad-tempered animal in all of Haven." Olivia took a small step back. "His spray is legendary, and I've been his victim more than once."

"We haven't threatened him, so there's no reason to…" The skunk spun around, lifted its tail, and before Zane could get them out of range, the animal sprayed. "Awww, shit."

Olivia coughed and turned, running for the side of the house. "I told you!"

"Where are you going?"

"We've got to get out of these clothes and shower!"

Feeling his eyes water, he glared at the offending animal. "That was uncalled for."

"Are you coming?" Olivia called out.

"On my way," He jogged to the side of the house and watched Oliva throw open a curtain to an impressive outdoor shower. "Nice setup. May have to add something like that to the Hawker homestead."

"Why are you standing there, Zane? Get out of your clothes."

"I can just..." Brain sputtering, he tried not to let his jaw fall to the ground as Olivia's T-shirt flew over her head. "So many tempting slopes and valleys."

"What?"

"Nothing, I should get home and..."

"The longer you leave it, the harder it is to get rid of."

"You sure you ready to see that much of me?"

Olivia rolled her eyes and began peeling off her jeans. "Jeeze, Zane, you're not the first naked man I've ever seen. I mean...I'm a medical illustrator, after all. I know more about the human body than most, and," she swallowed, "your parts are probably a little bigger, is all."

"A lot bigger," he mumbled as inch by delectable inch of Liv's mouth-watering curves were slowly revealed. If he managed not to take a bite out of her juicy ass before the day was done, it would be a damn miracle. He dug up the last scraps of control he could get ahold of and told himself that behaving was within his grasp. "I'm taking you at your word, Liv. And pray that you know what you're doing."

He pulled his shirt over his head and heard a sharp intake of breath. His gaze flew to hers, and he decided the flush covering her cheeks meant that God believed in fair play. "You okay, babe?"

"Sure, why wouldn't I be?" Her hand fluttered. "Not anything I haven't seen before."

He flicked the top button on his jeans and bit back a smile when her fingers flew to her mouth. "Good to know." Not one to let a tactical advantage go to waste, he slowly flicked each of the remaining buttons open. "You're looking a little flushed."

"Am not!"

The force or her rebuttal told him that the ball was still in play. "Okay, Liv. If you say so." He tipped his chin toward the waterspout. "Do you think we should turn the water on?"

"Oh, yeah…sure." Never letting her gaze move off-target, she twisted the lever. "It'll be warm in a minute."

"Excellent," he replied, peeling his jeans off slowly.

"Oh…"

His eyes flew up. "What?"

"Nothing, I would've just guessed boxers, not briefs."

He flicked his jeans into the pile of discarded clothes. "Most days I go commando; I guess it's your good luck that today wasn't one of them."

"Or bad luck," she murmured.

Not able to keep his happiness under wraps for a second longer, he took her hand and stepped into the shower. "Luck can change on a dime, so you never know what good fortune lay ahead."

The pulse beating against her neck told him that she might just agree.

\*\*\*

Apparently, the universe had been listening to her earlier entreaty, and she was about to be given exactly what she asked for.

Ready or not.

Mentally slapping herself upside the head, she reluctantly admitted that it was all but impossible to keep Zane's earlier offenses top of mind. Could she blame it on his spectacular body looming so close?

Her shoulders sagged, and she silently acknowledged that all it took for her to forgive rejection was a set of massive shoulders, strong legs, and…a package that was quite impressive.

Big dick energy, indeed.

Not that she was looking.

But good Lawd, it was kinda hard not to.

"Liv…"

"Mmmm?"

"You okay?"

"Of course," she sputtered, hoping he couldn't read the dirty thoughts crowding her brain. "Other than being bathed in the foulest smell, I'm right as rain."

"Well, I'm not."

Not able to resist the uncertainty in his voice, she looked up. "Really…why?"

"Because I don't know how to turn back time." He slowly ran his finger down the slope of her shoulder. "I'm standing in front of the most desirable woman I've ever encountered. Nearly naked. And I can't do a damn thing about it because I listened to the damn demons in my head that said I wasn't ready. Or sane enough."

"Oh, Zane…"

"If I could take back the words, I would."

She told herself not to make more of the moment than there was. He was probably just experiencing a raging case of lust, just like she was. "It's fine…"

"No, it sure as hell isn't."

The sincerity in his tone made fingers of heat bloom below her belly button. "I came on strong and…" Seeing his head lower and mouth hover made the rest of her sentence disappear. She held her breath as his lips almost grazed hers.

"Liv, you think you might ever give me a second chance?"

"At what?"

"Us," he said quietly.

The idea of there being a *them* made her brain stutter. And when his lips brushed hers, the list of reasons why they would never work flew from her head.

"Yes," he said against her mouth. "I'd like a shot at seeing if this crazy thing running between us is the real deal."

"As in a real disaster?" She filled her lungs with air. "I think a short lusty escapade that will leave us both satisfied and relatively unscathed is a much better option."

"Yeah, that's not going work for me 'cause once we turn on the tap, it's likely going to be near impossible to shut off."

"You never know." She framed his mouth with her hand and nipped his bottom lip. "We might just spend a couple of hours tearing up the sheets and never need to be in one another's company again."

"You think that's all it's gonna take?" He let his blunt finger graze along her rib cage and then move over the lace decorating her almost sheer bra.

"Maybe." Heart hammering in furious beats, desire blurred her vision as Zane moved his hands confidently across her skin.

Was he about to lose his manners?

A hungry mouth and uncompromising touch told her yes.

Could he be the one to welcome her hidden desires? The ones she'd kept an incredibly tight leash on. The ones that included wild, messy sex. Bared teeth and pulled hair?

A thing so raw and real that it would stain her skin until the end of time.

"You think you can deal with the fire between us?" he asked quietly.

She splayed her hands on his chest and stepped back, trying to slow her galloping heart. "I don't think it's me that we need to worry about." She dug her nails into the slab of muscle that covered his chest. "After all, I'm not the one who ran away." Zane's lush mouth pinched, and she didn't think yelling checkmate would be welcome.

"I'm gonna give you that one, but need to know if that was a yes or a no. Because I need a clear answer before I let myself off the leash and imprint my body on yours."

Hunger bled from his words, and her cool vanished. She stepped close enough for their feet to touch. "I suppose fooling around wouldn't be the worst way to spend the afternoon."

"Not by a long shot."

Keeping their eyes locked, she accepted that gravity had been pushing her toward him from the moment they met. Squeaking, she felt his large, warm hands lift her like a leaf and deposit her carefully on the small bench. "What are you doing? We have to scrub off the stink."

"In a minute," he gritted out. "I need to get my mouth on you and give you a proper hello."

Going soft and wet between her legs, a short hysterical giggle escaped.

Biology was so simple and damning.

Zane dropped to his knees. Overwhelmed and deliriously happy, she rested her hands on his shoulders. "Kiss me already."

"Or what?" he rasped out.

"I'll turn the tables."

"You think something like that is possible?"

She bit her bottom lip, looked down, and wondered if Zane's briefs were going to be any match for the erection straining against the soaked material. "Without a doubt. And I'm betting once it happens, you'll have no choice but to do as I say."

"Guess we'll see."

Zane took her mouth in a savage kiss and then made sure his thick erection was in the perfect position to slide up the valley of her parted legs, hitting her clit perfectly. "Oooohhh."

"What were you saying?"

"Don't know," she moaned, knowing that letting him have his way for a minute would be best.

\*\*\*

A rare satisfaction filled Zane's chest the moment Olivia returned his kiss, making the mental gymnastics he'd done about not needing her disappear.

Not sure if he was a decent kisser or not, he pushed a little and decided that her lips opening under his insistence was a good sign. He slid his tongue home and let the sound of her whimpers soothe his out-of-control need.

His mouth was punishing.

But she handled it.

She let his tongue stroke and play. Submitted.

Why did he suddenly need to control?

He'd never cared before.

But everything with Olivia was different.

Her fingers dug into his shoulders, sending a ripple of satisfaction shooting down his back. Needing more, he dragged his lips between her breasts and gave each nipple a graze of his teeth through the thin silk of her bra. Her short moans filled the steamy enclosure and her back arched, making the invitation irresistible.

Back and forth, he made a feast of her delicious flesh. "Addictive."

He skated his stubbled chin across her belly and took note of the red streak it left behind. Impatient to mark her further, he moved lower and couldn't wait to get his mouth on her most intimate spot.

To get her taste imprinted on his memory.

"Zane...what are you doing?"

He ran his tongue along his lip. "I'm going to eat you up until your honey runs down my chin, and your voice fills the air with my name."

Olivia's eyes widened. "Oh...well...okay."

He let the anticipation straining his muscles free as he ripped her panties and spread her legs open. Pink and wet. And all his. A growl escaped, and he bent down, licking from back to front in one long swipe.

"Ohhhhh, Zane."

*Damn right!* He pushed his middle finger into her channel and bit the inside of his cheek, thinking of the tightness that awaited him. "Mine now."

"I don't know if..."

"Mine," he repeated, untucking his finger from her warmth. He pushed his tongue through the slick sweetness of her folds and let his tongue hit her tiny nub. Lapping, again and again, he didn't stop. Hips moving like an ocean wave, Olivia pushed herself closer to his working tongue.

One long sweet, keening sound told him that she was about to peak, and he felt cum leaking from his cock. Pride filled his chest as she gave in to the orgasm. He kept his mouth where it was and did what he could to stretch her release as far as he could. His name a prayer on her lips, she repeated it as she collapsed. A silly smile filled her face, and he moved up her body, kissing her fully on the mouth. "I love that damn skunk."

Olivia responded by taking his face and kissing him firmly. His chest ached in response, along with his dick. Momentarily spun out, he couldn't believe this beautiful woman was into him.

"Is it my turn?" Olivia asked lazily. "I want to get my mouth on you and make you my slave.

"You don't have…" The sound of a car approaching interrupted him, and he stood. "Expecting anyone?"

"No," she squeaked before standing.

A car door slammed. "Olivia, darling. I brought you some delicious peaches."

"That's my grandmother."

Zane lifted Olivia to her feet as the sound of footsteps approached. "Well, this is gonna be interesting."

"Darling, what is that awful smell?"

Olivia pulled a corner of the curtain open. "Hi, Grams."

"Oh, my. Am I responsible for coitus interruptus?"

Olivia burst into giggles and whipped the curtain closed. "Go inside, Grams. We'll be there shortly."

"Don't rush on my account. I'll make some snacks and martinis."

Zane let go of a frustrated chuckle. "Does this mean we're having drinks with Margret?"

"Seems so," Olivia said as she bit back more laughter. "And you get to do it in a towel."

"Lucky for you two, I've got a go-bag in my truck and have a change of clothes."

Olivia reached around his large frame and grabbed the bottle of soap. "I don't know if either of us would call that lucky."

Zane slid his hand under the strap of Olivia's bra. "Raincheck."

"Maybe."

"Just know that I'll not relent until you give me a hell yeah." He kissed her full mouth and then took the soap out of her hand. "Spin around, babe; I'm gonna get you cleaned up."

"Bossy."

"You have no idea."

"Just know that the years you spent commanding a bunch of Green Berets in no way prepared you to deal with the likes of me."

"Never thought different." Letting a rare smile form, he gave into the happiness that was trying to find a place to land.

Fighting gravity didn't seem worth the effort anymore.

## CHAPTER ELEVEN

Olivia lifted her almost empty glass and drained the remains of her martini as her grandmother chattered about the latest news from town.

Not that she or Zane had the slightest curiosity about the goings-on at the Paint and Sip. At least she assumed he wasn't interested despite the look of intent focus coloring his handsome features.

He was probably just being polite.

But what if he wasn't?

Was it possible that he gave women screaming orgasms regularly, and what he did in the shower was of no more significance than, say…the odd trip to the market? She glanced over with what she hoped was an expression of mild interest and tried to determine if the intimate act had affected him in any way.

The tick in his jaw could mean something. So could the slight bounce in his knee. Tearing her eyes away, she looked down and watched his hand cover hers.

"Olivia…"

Tuning back into the conversation, she looked between her grandmother and Zane. "Yes?"

"My goodness, dear. You've barely said a word since we sat down." Margret clucked her tongue. "Perhaps I underestimated Zane's powers, and his fear of intimacy won't be quite the barrier we imagined."

"Wait, my fear of what?" Zane asked, sitting forward.

"Well, look at the time," Olivia said as she stood and wrestled the almost empty glass out of her grandmother's hand. "You should head back to town before it gets dark."

Margret laughed and kissed her granddaughter's cheek. "Good for you."

"Liv, you don't have to hustle Margret out. I'd love to hear all about what you two have been discussing."

"Grams needs to get home."

"I do," Margret said firmly. "I have the ladies coming over."

"Well, don't keep them waiting," Olivia interrupted, praying her grandmother would keep the details of their earlier conversations to herself. There was no need for Zane to know that she'd been talking about him with some regularity.

"You two will have to come to dinner this week."

"I'll call you," Olivia called out as Margret swanned out of the room. Nobody could make an entrance or an exit quite like the matriarch of the clan. The porch screen door slapped shut, and Oliva felt the muscles in her neck relax. "Well, I'm sure you want to be getting home."

"Not really," Zane said as he picked up the plate that held the remnants of the cheese and crackers. "We could make some dinner and…"

Olivia spun around and speed-walked toward the kitchen, wrestling with her second thoughts about getting involved with Zane. She set the glasses next to the sink and calculated the risk of heartbreak resulting from a short affair. How low did the number need to be before she moved forward?

"Are you having second thoughts?"

She accepted the plate and set it on the counter. "About what?"

"You and me." Zane lifted Olivia and set her on an empty section of the counter. "Are you still interested in giving me that raincheck?"

She closed her eyes. "Yes. As long as we don't talk too much."

"That's not real encouraging, Liv." He ran his thumb over her cheek. "Especially since you love nothing more than sharing your thoughts on everything great and small."

"Not anymore." She opened her eyes. "If we do talk, then there will be no doubt about our incompatibility. It might be best just to tear each other's clothes off and keep conversations to a minimum."

"Considering you're a chatterbox, I'm gonna say that's damn near impossible."

Olivia mimed zipping her mouth closed. "Bet I can find something better to do with my mouth." Zane's eyebrows shot sky high, and she laughed. "It's not that shocking?"

"Guess not, since you were discussing big-dick energy within days of meeting."

"Be that as it may…"

"Liv, just tell me what you want."

How did the man manage to be both menacing and romantic? She looked up, sensing there wasn't much difference between him and a wolf.

What would he do once she gave him the go-ahead? "I'd like…"

"Yes?" he asked, moving closer.

Feeling beautifully pinned by his massive body, she traced her finger lightly along the ropey muscles decorating his forearms. "To see what it looks like when you lose your manners."

"That can be arranged. But first, shouldn't we…"

"If you say talk again, know that I'll rescind my offer." Her heart traveled in a ricochet pattern as a growl erupted from his chest and his fingers flexed against her thighs. "A little meaningless sex never hurt anyone. And there's no reason to believe we'd be the exception."

"And that's where you'd be wrong." He slid his hand under the hem of her dress and gripped her thigh firmly. "But I'll save that discussion for another day."

She pressed her mouth to his. "I knew you'd see my way is best."

"For now," he murmured.

"Forever," she mumbled as his fingers slid inside her panties, making her lingering doubts disappear.

\*\*\*

The few social skills Zane possessed slipped away as Olivia moaned into his mouth. Why was their mating the one thing she didn't want to discuss? "Liv…"

"Zane, it doesn't have to be more than sex." She ran her finger over his jaw. "Maybe we just need to satisfy our curiosity. Get each other out of our systems."

"What if…"

Olivia shook her head. "Nope. We're going to ravage one another and hopefully do unspeakable things."

"But…"

"What we're *not* going to do is make it into more."

Zane slid his finger over her bundle of nerves and watched her eyes flutter closed. "You sure have a lotta rules, and I don't know that I'm interested in following them."

"Well, that's disappointing."

He arched an eyebrow as she shifted her hips. "Bet you'll get over it once my mouth is on you."

She leaned into his touch. "Or I get my mouth on you."

He let out a low chuckle. "We can save that for later."

Olivia hooked her leg around Zane's waist, drawing him closer. "You sure?"

"Yes!" He gathered her dress and pulled it over her head, hearing laughter spill out of her mouth. "Better." He gave her a dirty kiss and felt her small hands slide inside his shorts. "You want something?"

"You."

"Here?"

She pushed his shorts down his hips. "Yes!"

"You sure about this, Liv?" Her head bobbed in agreement, and he had no choice but to do as she asked. "Are you absolutely…"

"Why are you still talking?" She let out a huff. "You're supposed to be mindless with desire and unable to control yourself."

"Oh, don't you worry, woman. Control has left the premises." He bent down and teased a nipple through thin lace. "But any man who doesn't get a real clear hell yeah is a fool."

Olivia took his face and squished his cheeks together. "Zane Hawker, would you be kind enough to fu…"

"That's not a word that will ever describe what you and I do."

Olivia let out a sigh. "Well, that's disappointing."

"No, it's not." He dragged his teeth across her bottom lip. "We can do dirty things to each other all night long. But it's never going to be fucking."

"Okay," she wiggled out of her panties. "I'm ready."

"God damn." Feelings he couldn't name filled his chest as he pulled Olivia closer. He took a deep breath and slid his fingers inside her wet heat. "This for me?"

"Yes…"

"Good." He pushed his erection away from his stomach, slid it through Olivia's slick folds, and then eased inside. "God damn."

"Indeed," she said against his neck.

Her fingers dug into his shoulders, and he heard her take in a deep breath. "You feel so good, Olivia. I'm gonna drown in you."

"Yes," she said with a moan. "Drown together."

Was there anything sweeter than being enveloped in this woman's heat? Gritting his teeth, he willed himself to take his time. "Let's take this to the bedroom."

"No way," Olivia groaned, wrapping her legs around his waist. "I want counter sex."

He let out a rough groan, took her at her word, and gave her a feral thrust. She met him with a roll of her hips. "Wouldn't mind a little more room to work." Her gaze dropped to where they were joined, and she let out a little whimper when he worked himself out and then slowly back in.

"I…think…"

"I'm doing it wrong if you can still form a thought." He bent his head and let himself go. If she wanted dirty kitchen sex, then he was damn well going to deliver. He built up his pace, and the ancient dance began.

The beast and the beauty were a match, after all.

\*\*\*

Moaning into the most insane kiss of her life, Olivia wondered why a grumpy recluse was the one to light her world on fire.

Doing what she could to turn off the doubtful voice, she focused on the man's magic. Who cared if three days ago he wanted no part of her? Today, he did, and she wanted to wring every delicious drop of satisfaction that she could.

Physical pleasure hadn't been a part of her life for far too long, and she needed to savor every naughty second. The sound of Zane's possessive growl knocked away her thoughts, and she let lust whip through her veins. "You are…"

"Making you incredibly happy?" he finished as he lifted his head.

His gaze was coated with a hunger she wasn't entirely prepared for. Had anyone ever looked at her with that kind of desire?

Raw lust and something so unmistakably sweet clawed at her defenses, and she tugged on his arms until their faces were close. "Yes."

"We're only getting started."

She bit back a smile and reveled in the bite of his tone. *This*, she thought, is what I've been waiting for.

To be consumed.

Desired wholly.

Looking into his eyes made words she couldn't utter brush against the inside of her throat. She mentally swept away the sentiments and focused on the blunt finger pressing against her clit. If this was how she was meant to lose her mind, then so be it.

Her stomach shuddered, and she cupped his jaw, watching his long lashes brushing against his cheek. The way he made her feel…how had he managed to make her body a servant to his?

Touchable masculinity.

That's what the man who was playing her body like an instrument had.

Every thrust made her body pulse.

She gripped his incredible ass with both hands and tried to bring him closer.

The word more ran in a loop across her mind, and one particularly well-placed thrust had her keening. "Zaaaaaaane…"

"Going to hit that spot a hundred more times, babe."

His pelvis ground against her heat. Harder. Deeper. The world shimmered, and her body began to shake. Everything she thought she knew about sex and pleasure flew out the window. "I'm going to…"

"Do it!" He cupped her head and pressed it against his chest. "I want you to shatter into a million pieces."

Emotions exploded—sudden and intense.

"Zane."

"I got you, Liv."

Her body began to dissolve along with a couple of hard-won defenses. How had he managed it? One last drive of his body set off her release. Pleasure spiraled as he unleashed the last of his assault.

Hanging on for dear life, she gave in to the pleasure blackout and heard Zane's roar of release.

How had she underestimated him?

## CHAPTER TWELVE

Zane walked into Olivia's studio and added the elegant line of her neck to the growing list of attributes he found fascinating. A *list* that told him he was in the deepest kind of trouble. Two days had passed since they'd become intimate, and his hunger for her company had taken on a life of its own.

Would he ever be satiated?

He cleared his throat and watched her turn with a happy smile. "Hey, Liv."

"Hi, Handsome."

He looked over his shoulder. "Who ya talking to?"

"You, silly!"

"When was the last time you had your eyes checked?"

"Two months ago." She bit her bottom lip. "And I have near-perfect vision."

"Don't know how that's possible," he muttered, gripping the door frame. "I wanted to let you know that I'll be in the yard working on the Ferris wheel."

Tipping her head, she frowned. "Well, that's disappointing." She stood and held out her hand. "I thought you came by to make out and...stuff."

He took her outstretched hand and pulled her into his chest. "Really?"

"Well, yeah."

Closing his eyes, he soaked in the pleasure of her touch. "Liv, you've got a deadline, and I...

"Can't wait another minute to do the naughty things we didn't get to the other night?"

"No!" He stepped back. "Don't distract me, woman."

She stepped forward. "Party pooper."

"That's not what you said when we were on round three."

"That was more than twenty-four hours ago." She pressed her hand against his chest. "The memory has faded, and I can barely recall what it felt like to have you…"

He covered her mouth. "You've got to have some mercy, babe." Looking up, he let out a groan. "I'm trying to do the right thing."

"Jumping each other is the right thing!" She let out a huff. "What's the point of having a sexy neighbor if you can't take advantage of it on the odd Wednesday afternoon?"

Unchartered territory was the only way to describe his current situation. "I thought we were supposed to do stuff with our clothes on so we can build a relationship. Why are you trying to thwart my efforts?"

"Relationship?"

He ignored the disappointment that tried to bloom. "Said with the same enthusiasm as tax preparation." Lifting her hand, he pressed a kiss to it. "I thought that word would've been met with a shit-ton more enthusiasm." Her mouth pinched into a firm line, and he didn't know why the idea of them communicating with words and not their bodies was so unappealing. "Talk to me, Liv. What's going on in that mind of yours?"

"It's just that…"

Holding himself still, he tried not to assume the worst.

126

Had he said too much? Too little?

The rules were a mystery, and he felt exposed. A feeling that was never welcome.

"I don't want to make more of it than there is." She ran her hand over his T-shirt. "I think we're best suited for a fling."

"Are you saying that because you're protecting yourself or because you have no desire to get to know me?" An unnamed feeling kicked up in his gut. Was this what vulnerability felt like?

"I'm not going to pick up the scissors and make myself smaller."

Lifting her chin, he studied the concern in her eyes. "I'm not asking you to do that."

"You said I was a complication." Stepping back, she twisted her hands together. "And you weren't interested in my chaos. Which certainly suggests that you'd like to see a tamer version," she groused. "Which, for the record, is not available."

"I like the full 3-D version of you." He lifted her into his arms and collapsed on the small couch. "I got spooked because trying and failing can be soul-shattering, and let's face it, mine is still in pieces."

"You're not the only one who is Scotch-taped together." She ran her fingers over his scars. "Just because I don't bear physical marks doesn't mean that I'm not fragile too."

"You seem indomitable."

"Well, I'm not. I just put on a better show than you."

He picked at a loose string on her shorts. "I'm about the worst bet there is Liv. My mental health is sketchy at best, and my experience in making another human happy is all but non-existent." The tension in her muscles eased. "I'd like to keep the door open, though, and see if hanging out together could lead to something."

"Why?" she asked, covering his hand. "What made you change your mind?"

"You make me want to do better. And I think that's got to mean something." He fixed the silk bow in her hair. "I want to touch more than your body, Liv."

"Really?"

"Yes. I'd like to earn the privilege of hearing your stories." Dipping his head, he let his mouth rest against hers. "The good ones." He kissed her slowly. "And the hard ones." Her hand fisted into his T-shirt. "I'm trying to get comfortable with uncertainty. I figure most people are just winging it and trying to mitigate the risks. Waiting until you know how things are going to work out is a coward's play. And believe it or not, that's not what I am."

"Are you suggesting a leap of faith?" she whispered.

"Yeah. A big ass jump into the unknown." He covered her hand, praying for a positive response. "What do you think?"

"I suppose we could hang out for a while."

"Okay." He kissed her head and told himself to take the win. "That's good, Liv."

Real good.

\*\*\*

Olivia rested her head against Zane's chest and didn't know what to make of the latest plot twist. Why was he making noise about a relationship? It simply didn't make sense since several days ago he wanted no part of her.

Mentally stomping on the tiny hope that tried to unfurl, she knew that his tune would change the minute their sexual chemistry fizzled. Something she expected to happen within a matter of days.

Unless her grumpy warrior was capable of the best magic trick of all.

No, that was too unlikely to contemplate. He certainly wasn't going to be the one to give her the inexpressible comfort of feeling safe. Zane Hawker was the last man on earth who'd allow her the luxury of having to neither weigh thoughts nor measure words.

Laughing silently, she knew that any man who said leave me alone one minute and let's go for it the next wasn't likely to stick around and make the investment necessary. He was clearly swimming in happy sex hormones, and before too long, would be sated. Feeling mildly satisfied with the explanation, she listened to the clock tick and mentally poked at the familiar dull pain in her chest.

*How much does it still hurt?* A question she'd asked herself nearly every day of the last five years. One of the therapists she'd seen early on said it was a coping mechanism that survivors utilized—a way not to forget.

Should she share the story with Zane?

Would he be interested in the event that shaped her into who she was today?

She'd been poking, prodding, and picking at his story since they'd met and he could very well feel the need to return the favor at some point.

Not because he genuinely wanted to know her, of course. But because giving up useful intel wasn't what an operator did. And despite some evidence to the contrary, he was still very much a soldier.

Why had she been so insistent on asking a hundred questions?

Sucking in a breath, she realized it was because she wanted to know him. In every way. A thing that hadn't happened since Thad. A dull pain spiked in her chest with the admission, and she twisted her fingers together.

Zane sat up. "You feel like telling me about whatever made you stiffen and suck in a breath?"

*Darn it!*

She loosened her limbs and pushed her mouth into a smile. "I'm just excited about the prospect of bringing the Ferris wheel back to life."

"You didn't put any effort into that lie, so try again."

"I should get back to work." She heaved herself off his lap and felt a large hand land on her leg. "Lots to do."

He arched an eyebrow. "And yet, five minutes ago, you wanted to spend hours doing dirty things to one another."

"Mutually satisfying physical relations between consenting adults isn't dirty."

"Unless it's done right." He tugged her hand.

Knowing he had the tenacity of a bull and the patience of a Siberian tiger, she turned slowly and silently cursed his flashing eyes. "The ride won't fix itself."

Zane stood. "Something has you spooked, and the sooner I know what it is, the better."

"For whom?"

He lifted a picture off the bookcase. "I'm guessing it has something to do with this."

She watched him study the photo and knew there was no mistaking how much the man in the picture meant to her. "That's Thad. We were college sweethearts and completely in love."

"Were?" Zane asked quietly.

"Yes." She looked down at the worn wooden floor. "We were driving home from grad school with our lives stretched out before us with a hundred possibilities. We had so many plans." The familiar boulder of pain moved slightly in her chest. "We were hit by a drunk driver." She closed her eyes. "Bones crushed. Organs twisted into something unrecognizable." Tears threatened to spill, and she swallowed loudly. "I survived. Thad didn't."

Zane set the picture down carefully, and she tried to fill her lungs with air. "He had a ring in his bag."

"I'm so sorry, Liv."

"I don't think you get more than one great love. He was likely mine." Twisting her rings, she breathed slowly. "There wasn't a part of me that he didn't accept. Every quirk, foible, and annoying habit. He took it all in stride and loved me with every bone in his body."

Zane's features tightened, and she took his outstretched hand. "Sounds like a tragedy, doesn't it?"

"Sure does."

"It's not. Some people don't get one shot at that kind of happiness." His long fingers covered hers. "I decided long ago to appreciate what I had and make the most of surviving the accident."

"I had a feeling there was a reason."

"For what?"

"You're a tornado of gratitude and happiness." Lifting her hand, he folded it in his. "That usually doesn't happen unless you survived something horrific."

She glanced up. "Does that mean I should see your storm of positivity soon since you're a survivor too?"

Cupping her cheek, he bit back a smile. "You never know what kind of miracles are in the offing."

Feeling lighter than she had in a long time, she was reminded that the world didn't stop spinning when she said the words aloud—when she talked about the man who showed her what love looked like. "You have a well of untapped kindness, Zane." A full smile broke across his handsome face, and nothing could've prepared her for how warm it made her feel.

"I knew this talking thing was a good idea."

"Talking naked is good too."

"You keep saying things like that, and I'm gonna think you're only interested in my body."

"You make it sound like a bad thing."

"Never count me out, Liv." He kissed her head. "Because I'm likely to surprise the hell out of you at some point."

"I look forward to it."

She rubbed her cheek against the soft cotton of his T-shirt and questioned why the phantom of love lost didn't seem to hang around when they were together. Was a second chance at happiness available down the road?

And was the man whose heart was beating against hers going to help her find it?

She closed her eyes and decided the idea was absurd.

\*\*\*

Lucy leaned against the screen door and shook her head. "Good Lord, does Zane wear that indecent smile every time he works on the disaster in your yard?"

Olivia handed her sister a glass of iced tea. "Not really." Heat bloomed in her lady bits, and she tried not to appear like a Cheshire cat.

"Oh, jeez…you sexed him up before I got here, and that's why he looks like a contented lion."

"Siberian tiger."

"What?"

"A Siberian tiger is the most patient animal in existence, and that's what Zane is." She sipped her tea. "Until he's not."

"If I weren't so happy for you, I'd be a tad bit jealous."

"Nothing to be envious about." She lifted her glass in Zane's direction. "This little entanglement has disaster written all over it." Closing her eyes, she let out a sigh. "The embers of hope flared earlier, but sadly are about to fizzle out."

"Who are you? My sister of immaculate positivity would never say anything like that."

"Reality is scratching at my door, and I'm not fool enough to ignore it for very much longer." She collapsed on the step. "Between Zane's PTSD, fear of intimacy, and desire to become the world's loneliest recluse and my near maniacal need to avoid complete devastation… we may only have another week of happiness, tops."

Lucy dropped down on the step and took a moment to arrange her full skirt. "What if…"

Olivia glanced at her sister. "Even my positivity can't come up with a happy ending."

"I assume you're planning to enjoy the ride for as long as you can then?"

"Yes."

"What about those pesky feelings you've never had before? How are you going to rationalize those away?"

"Still working on it."

"Any reason why you wouldn't simply give into them?"

Olivia looked into her sister's eyes. "Do you remember how long it took for me to function normally after Thad passed?"

"Of course."

"I have a feeling that if I allowed myself to fall in love with Zane, and he ran away in response, then the outcome would be far more devastating."

"Oh."

"But I'm not going to let that happen, so no need to worry." Olivia laced their hands together. "Enough about my nonsense. How are you?"

"Good."

"Why does that response scare me?" She swept Lucy's beautiful red hair over her shoulder. "You live life out loud and only use the word good when describing toast…or the dentist…or car repair."

"Peaceful. How's that?"

"If our sister Callie said it, then I'd say fantastic. But…it's you, and peaceful is not one of your favorite adjectives."

"But it could be." Lucy turned. "Maybe maturity is finally getting ahold of me, and the need to live on the edge is no longer as strong." She flattened her hands against her waist. "I'm thirty-two and don't need…"

"Yes, you do," Olivia said firmly. "Denying your true nature never lasts for long. Your purple-blue aura won't allow it."

"We'll see."

Olivia knew that saying more wouldn't change her sister's mind since no one was stronger willed. When Lucy set her mind to something, it was done…until she changed it. If she needed to pursue a more peaceful path for a while, then so be it. Though how it would last for longer than a week, she couldn't say.

She studied Zane in the distance, reminding herself that accepting the true nature of someone was best. No matter what messages your heart was sending.

What you see is what you got.

Not what you want.

## CHAPTER THIRTEEN

The sound of the front door creaking open was unexpected. Zane stomped out of the living room and felt a smile crack across his face when he saw Olivia. "I didn't know you were coming by."

She held up a quilted bag. "I couldn't be the only woman in town that hadn't brought you a casserole." Puckering her lips, she gave him a slow once over. "Especially since I'm the one who gets to see your naked glory."

"I don't think there's any glory in my nakedness."

"That's where you're wrong, sir." She dug her teeth into her bottom lip. "So very wrong."

"Guessing that mischievous glint means dessert will be served in the bedroom." He met her in the middle of the large hall and kissed her firmly before taking the bag from her hand. "Or any flat surface."

He felt her shiver and kissed her again. "And, for the record, only half the female population has graced the front steps, and almost everyone was hoping to run into Asher."

"Almost?" She stepped back with a frown.

The light from the leaded window threw a rainbow of color over Oliva, and he couldn't stop himself from running his finger slowly over her cheek.

How was this impossibly magnetic woman interested in his company? He couldn't make sense of it but also didn't want to question it too deeply since his focus had recently shifted in her direction.

"Zane..."

He blinked twice and realized he hadn't answered her question. "Yes?"

"Where did you go?" She rested her hand on his chest. "If you don't want to tell me what other beauties have caught your attention, you don't have to."

"Other beauties?" He took her hand and pulled her toward the kitchen. "We both know that's impossible and not just because I can barely handle you."

A disgruntled huff echoed down the hall, and he wondered if ignoring it would work. When another one followed, he stopped inside the kitchen. "Words, Olivia. Hit me with them, so I know what kind of tactical error I made."

She took the bag out of his hand and strode over to the island. "My goodness, Zane. You make it sound like being in my company requires a dog-eared copy of *The Art of War*."

"It kinda does," he mumbled quietly as he walked over to the fridge and pulled out a beer and a bottle of Olivia's favorite wine. And yes, he had stocked up. So what?

"How long before supper is ready?"

"Avoid and deflect. Are you sure that's necessary?"

"Yep." He grabbed a glass and filled it, deciding that Olivia needed a generous pour. "Here you go, babe."

She held up the glass. "Guess this is your way of telling me something."

"Not necessarily." He tilted his beer bottle against her glass and grinned. "I don't mind that little streak of jealousy you just showed since you tried to sell me the whole tryst thing the other day." Lifting the bottle to his mouth, he took a gulp. "We're both way outside our comfort zones, so the challenge of scaling a pile of doubt is daunting. No way around it."

"I'm surprised to hear you say that."

"Not sure why." He leaned against the island and watched her pull several containers out of the bag. "You experienced a crippling loss when Thad died and have no reason to risk your heart. And I'm gripping my PTSD from a half-dozen years as a Special Operator like it's my best friend. We're a shit-show in the making." The casserole dish thunked down on the counter, and he knew his brutal honesty might've been too much. "Did I miss anything?"

"No, and for the record, your pessimism and lack of faith don't make you any more immune to life's travails."

"Well aware of that." He stepped in, crowding her. "I have enough years on the frontlines to know that anything is possible." Lifting her chin, he gave her a soft kiss. "Including you and me finding a way to..."

"What?" she asked breathlessly.

"Be some kind of happiness for each other."

"Certainly not the worst option in the world."

Zane leaned back. "Love the enthusiasm."

"This from the man who sees clouds and assumes a tsunami is on its way."

He dug his fingers into her waist. "A man should be prepared for whatever storm is headed in his direction."

"Assuming I'm the troublesome weather pattern you're referring to."

"Nothing wrong with having a tempest in your life." The sound of something crashing reverberated against the ceiling and Zane looked up. "It's either my dead relatives weighing in or a critter that got into one of the open windows."

Olivia turned toward the doorway. "Well, let's go investigate. I'm dying to get acquainted with the Hawker spirits."

"You say that like it's possible." He took Olivia's hand and headed toward the staircase. "And normal."

"It's not abnormal, and if they like you, they could very well enjoy my company too!"

"No doubt about it," he mumbled as they climbed the stairs together. Because he sure as hell enjoyed her and couldn't see it changing any time soon.

God help them both.

\*\*\*

Olivia stepped into the enormous attic and noticed a chair had been tipped over. Was it the work of a bored spirit or a critter that had made a home in the dusty space?

"It's a lot of junk, isn't it?" Zane asked.

"It's a lot of treasure."

Zane closed a window and then dusted off his hands. "Which tells you everything about our world views."

"Not necessarily," she replied as she walked over to a chest and pulled open a drawer. "You should let the Haven Ladies' Society up here. They'd have this stuff sorted and archived within a week."

"Are they like the Freemasons?"

"I suppose. Both require an invitation and have elaborate secret ceremonies. Most of the women over the age of fifty are members, and, according to my grandmother, their main goal is to improve the community."

"Have any idea what that entails?"

"Nope, and they're a tight-lipped group. The few tidbits I've managed to collect suggest they orchestrate things that need to be done. How all that is managed is a mystery that won't be solved until I gain membership."

"Interesting." Zane flicked through several pictures and then looked up. "I wouldn't mind hearing the backstory on the folks that haven't been able to cross over."

"Then let's host a séance."

"Can't we just get some of the old birds to spill?"

She rolled her eyes. "Why bother when we have our very own medium who can communicate with the other side directly?"

"I was hoping there might be another way to find out what's keeping them here."

She strolled over to an open trunk. "When I moved into my house, I had a lovely spirit that visited on occasion."

"Really?"

"Oh, yes. I made sure to have a séance right away, so we could get acquainted. It seems it wasn't a matter of her not wanting to pass to the other side, but more of a desire to stay. Bea always says that there are many planes in which to travel, and occasionally, a spirit isn't done with this one."

"Well, I have more than a few who've decided to stay put."

"The one who visited me didn't want to leave her memories behind. She had raised a family in the house and couldn't stand to be away."

Zane stroked his cheek. "Mr. Ford, the old caretaker, never mentioned seeing any of the spirits, and I'm not sure why my presence is making them so lively."

"Bea told me that moving furniture around, renovations and such, can cause spirit roommates to make themselves known."

"You'd think they'd be happy with the changes and leave me in peace." He lifted his gaze and stared out the window. "Instead, they're rattling, slamming, and otherwise causing a ruckus."

"Maybe they're trying to keep you company while you give the whole silly hermit thing a whirl."

Zane pulled a wooden boat out of the box and studied it. "It's possible. But I'm guessing it has more to do with having a Hawker in residence. I might be the first one to inhabit this old manse in twenty years."

"Do you see them?" Olivia asked.

"I feel them and occasionally get a glimpse of …"

"What?" She took his hand and moved closer.

"A feature, or a piece of clothing. It's hard to explain."

"I miss my spirit. You're lucky to have so many."

Zane put the boat back in the box. "I don't feel fortunate."

"I enjoyed the company and wish I had one that visited more often." She lifted a scarf and ran it through her hands.

"I'd be more than happy to send some of the more troublesome your way. More than one of them would get a kick out of you."

"If only that were possible." She let out a long sigh. "I might have the wrong energy."

"You're light and goodness, so I don't see how that's possible. Why they want to hang out with my cranky ass is not something I'm ever going to understand." He shrugged. "Perhaps they like tussling with my demons."

"And why do you allow those pesky bastards to hang around?"

"If the Army psych is to be believed, it's because I can't forgive myself for failing—for not bringing the men home I was entrusted with." He ran his hand over a stack of pictures. "For the lives I took and the ones I didn't. You live on the front lines for any amount of time, and you are bound to come home with more than a few regrets." He bent his head. "I don't know how the ledger is going to come out when I stand at the pearly gates, but I'm praying that I did more good than bad."

"I suppose that's all any of us hope for."

"True. But I had more of a chance to land on the wrong side. Most days, I'm convinced I failed."

"The fact that you stood between good and evil tells me that you did no such thing."

"Guess time will tell."

"Are you getting hungry?" She stepped back. "I brought you a feast."

Zane moved closer. "Any chance of me feasting on you first?" He took her hand and pulled her into his chest. "I've been working on the master bath and think you might like what I've done."

She pulled his head down and rested her lips against his lush mouth. "Oh, yeah..."

"Yeah."

He took her mouth in a feral kiss of possession, and she had never wanted to give in to a man more. Zane Hawker was all the colors, all the dangerous emotions, and everything that didn't make sense. If he had a blinking sign over his head, it would read: danger ahead, turn back now.

Which is exactly what she should do because the only way she'd survived losing Thad was by living small.

Not wanting much.

Risking nothing.

"You done fighting with yourself?" Zane asked against her mouth.

"I wasn't..."

He pulled away from the kiss. "Tell me, Liv."

"You scare the hell out of me." She looked down. "I've never been one to walk into the fire, but you make me want to do exactly that. There's a part of me that wants to smother you in sexy vibes and possibilities. But the sane part knows that backpedaling it to the nearest exit would be best."

"Why would you want," he kissed her leisurely, "less of this?"

"Because you're likely lethal to my long-term sanity."

He rested their heads together. "Just know that I'm having the same struggle but am trying not to obliterate my first chance at happiness."

She took his face in her hands. "I'm never ready for your surprising sentiments."

"Join me on the edge of reason, Liv. And let's see if we can beat the odds."

"I don't like the edge, Zane."

"But that's where the good stuff is." He pressed their bodies together. "Do you feel like checking out the clawfoot tub in my bathroom?"

Grabbing his hand, she headed toward the staircase. "I want to check you out...naked...in the tub."

A low rumble of laughter echoed off the wood rafters, and she knew it was a sound she would remember for a long time to come.

No matter how things turned out.

\*\*\*

Few things in life made Zane's hands shake. And even fewer things that made him wish he had some sort of poetic talent.

Olivia standing before him with a blazing smile made both of those rare occurrences possible.

Unbuttoned.

Unzipped.

And free of everything that separated them made him want to fall to his knees and utter beautiful words of appreciation. He held out his hand instead and was grateful when she took it without hesitation. "I know there's something I should say...to let you know...that I like where things are headed."

She took a step back and laughed before stepping into the tub filled with bubbles. "I don't know that a sexy romp needs any sort of declaration, but if you want to throw out a funny quip, I wouldn't be opposed."

"Not sure I have one that's worthy." He followed her and sank into the water, making a fair bit of it slosh over the side. "Might need to be less aggressive the next time I fill it."

Oliva ran her hand over the water. "I like it. More is better."

He leaned back against the rim and told himself that a bubble bath with his girl was no big deal. So what if he'd never done it? It didn't mean he couldn't learn how. Just like the hundreds of skills he developed being on the front lines. He could blow up just about anything…certainly, there was something in that skill set that could be used in what he and Oliva were attempting. "What I was trying to say earlier was…"

"I'm naked, Zane." She crawled up his body. "Seduction isn't required since I'm kind of a sure bet."

He pushed his hands through the water, gripping her hips. "You sure make it hard to be romantic."

"That wasn't my intent."

"I have no idea what the hell I'm doing." Gritting his teeth, he looked over her shoulder. "If this were as simple as inserting tab A into tab B and both of us getting off, then I would be fine. But…"

"It feels like more, and neither of us knows what to do?"

He brought her head against his and closed his eyes. "Yes."

"Are you saying a short, dirty tryst without an ounce of complications is nothing more than a poorly thought-out fantasy?"

"Yeah," he said quietly. "And you have no idea how much it pisses me off."

"Same," Olivia said quietly. "I was so hoping you'd break my dirty affair cherry and then disappear in the morning mist."

"We don't get a morning mist, babe."

"I know," she replied as she lifted her head. "It's just a fantasy I carry around because I watched *Pride and Prejudice* one too many times."

"So…"

Olivia wiggled around and then lifted her eyes. "Should we just have dirty sex, eat the casserole, and then swear to stay away from one another?"

Snorting, he shifted his hips. 'Yeah, like that's gonna work."

"It could." She lifted herself on her knees and looked down. "But we'd have to do it twice."

Zane fisted his erection and shifted Olivia so she was a breath away from making his world right. "Maybe we should round it up to three, just to make sure."

"Yeah," she murmured. "Five seems like a reasonable number."

"Just to be clear, I'm not gonna get blowback when I leave a couple of teeth marks, right?"

"Nope." She flicked his hand away and guided him into her heat. "Not at all."

Lust drove his next move as a roar filled his ears, and he gave into the fact that there wasn't a sin he wouldn't commit to have Liv in his life. And not just naked in the tub.

Tab A, Tab B, his ass. Their physical connection was on a different level.

Olivia stroked his cheek with her thumbs. "Yes, Zane."

"To what exactly?"

"Everything."

Biting back a vile curse, he did his best not to blackout as Olivia's tight heat welcomed him. "Feel that?"

Dragging her mouth across his collarbone, she nipped his skin. "Yes."

"Me too." His heart vibrated like a tuning fork as his body moved like the raging ocean. Lifting his gaze, he was instantly pinned by Liv's beautiful eyes. "Everywhere," he grunted. "I feel you everywhere."

"I've got you," she said, her nails digging into his skin. "Stay with me."

"Always." Her warm breath coasted across his face. Head to toe, there wasn't a part of him that wasn't sensitized to her presence.

His need spun out as the sound of her hips slapping against the water bounced off the tile. Rational thought vanished, and she stilled. He slid his hand between their bodies and sent her over the edge. Joining her a moment later, he gritted out her name, his muscles jerking as he released his seed.

A rare satisfaction brushed across his soul, and he had a bad feeling that she was the woman who was going to either ruin him or give him every happiness that he didn't deserve.

## CHAPTER FOURTEEN

The next day, Zane ambled down Main Street with Olivia and decided that their liaison having a better than fifty-fifty chance of making Chernobyl look like a children's party wasn't that big of a deal.

A fact he should share with the last army psych he saw, if only because it would make her feel like he'd put some of her wise counsel into practice. Mentally giving himself a high-five, he knew that holding hands with a woman in public was some damn fine mental health.

"Zane…"

"Yeah, babe?"

"Did you hear my question?"

"Sorry I missed it." He closed one eye. "I was…

"Making a pro and con list?"

"No," he sputtered.

"I find that hard to believe," she ran her eyes over him slowly, "since you appeared to be convincing yourself to stay on the right side of things, so you'd have a shot at every single one of your dirty ideas."

He slowed their pace. "Liv, we both know you're a lot naughtier than me."

"Just because I've done some research on the benefits of a sex swing in no way suggests that I possess more deviant proclivities." She let out a disgruntled huff.

"Well aware of that." Pulling her under a flowering plum tree, he tipped her chin. "Can you repeat the question?"

She batted her eyelashes. "I forgot."

"No, you didn't." Doing the unthinkable, he bent down and kissed her. He'd never been one to put his personal life on blast, but damn if he could stop himself from showing the woman his affection.

A word he would've sworn he was incapable of using.

"Too bad they don't come in a size that would accommodate us."

He laughed against her mouth and knew she was yanking his chain since audacity was her middle name. "I'm fairly competent at rigging things together, so never say never."

She pressed their mouths together and then stepped back. "I'll keep that in mind."

"Please do." He tilted his head toward the coffee shop. "You ready for lunch?"

"Yes, please."

He led her toward the door, knowing that most people will get you all wrong, and someone getting you right was as good a thing there was in the world. Why God decided that Olivia was going to be the person, he couldn't say.

Zane thanked the waitress and then watched Olivia unfold a napkin. "You're thinking pretty loud there, babe. Do you have anything to share?"

"I think we've moved to the second stage."

"Of what?" Zane asked as he pushed the plate of onion rings in her direction.

"There are four stages of attraction, and I think we're progressing to the next one."

"Can I assume that means you've given up the idea of a tryst and have decided to join me on the ledge?"

"Let's just say I'm giving the idea some strong consideration." She dunked an onion ring in the ranch dressing and then popped it into her mouth. "But don't get too excited because, despite the initial mad rush I made you endure, I have a pile of reservations."

"I assumed as much." He took her hand and ignored the slice of frustration in his chest, knowing his freak out had put doubt in Olivia's mind. "So, what is the next stage anyway?"

"Mutual admiration. It's when two people have chemistry and have decided to do something with it." She covered his hand. "The first stage is attraction. Either physical or emotional. The third stage is when people decide to make a go of it. See if they can flourish."

"And the fourth?"

"Compatibility. When a couple discovers they function well together." She tilted her head. "I don't think all that many people make it to the final stage."

"Did you get there with Thad?" He watched her brows drop and knew it was a shit question. It wasn't any of his business. "You don't have to answer."

"My goodness, a question like that makes me think you mean all the lovely things you've said and really do intend to get to know me." She pursed her lips. "I must be way better at sex than I thought. Maybe I can become a vixen after all."

"You already are, woman." He watched her bat her eyelashes and found a rusty chuckle escaping.

"If you want to tell me the things you enjoyed most, I wouldn't mind."

"Why?" he asked sharply.

"Because knowing one's strengths and building on them is never a bad idea."

A picture of her honing those skills for someone else made a knife of jealousy slide through his gut. How the hell had he become possessive? "I'll get right on it."

Olivia picked up her sandwich. "No, you won't."

"You never answered my question."

She set her sandwich down. "Yes, Zane. I was connected to Thad in all ways. He was my first love and the man I thought I would spend my life with." Her shoulders sagged. "But that's not how things worked out."

"I've never been tempted to give into chemistry or anything else with a woman. Being deployed made it all but impossible, and truth be told, it was a great excuse never to put myself out there."

"Is there a *but* coming?"

He snorted. "I'm not a complete asshole." He watched her beautiful eyebrow arch. "You are changing my SOP."

"Standard Operating Procedure?"

"I see someone has been on Google."

"Are you impressed?" she asked with a wide smile.

"Always. And yeah, you have changed my SOP, and I don't have a clue what to do about it."

"Might as well give in." She leaned in and kissed his cheek. "If only for a little while. I don't think we'll last the month, but that doesn't mean we shouldn't make the most of it."

"You sure love to put a time stamp on things."

"I know how perilous an attachment with you could be and want to get out before complete devastation occurs." She hitched her shoulder. "A woman only has so much Scotch tape, and a heart broken twice won't have a chance at a third."

"You saying that's possible?"

"Yes, Zane. I am."

Before he could say more, one of the owners stopped at the table, refilling their glasses. Was she as scared of him as he was of her? He rolled the possibility over in his mind and decided the idea was ludicrous.

"Zane?"

He looked between the women. "What did I miss?"

Grace patted his shoulder. "Nothing earth-shattering. I just wanted to know how the renovations are going."

"Slow." He closed one eye as the sun cut through the large window and bounced off the woman's sparkly sweatshirt. "Which is to be expected from a three-story stone manse that hasn't been touched in years."

"We sure do you miss your grandmother at our meetings. She was such a bright light of the Haven Ladies' Society. I tell you; no one could concoct a better scheme than Nan Hawker."

"Scheme?" Olivia asked, sitting forward. "What kind of intrigues are we talking about exactly?"

Grace pursed her lips. "It's not called a secret society for nothing, young lady." She patted her gray curls. "The only thing I can say is that we've cooked more than one lying, cheater's goose but good. And anyone who was in possession of the same facts would've done the same thing."

"Interesting," Olivia replied, squeezing Zane's hand. "And whose goose specifically was cooked?"

"Oh, I better get back to the kitchen; my wife is giving the signal. Enjoy your lunch."

Zane chuckled when he saw Liv's displeased expression. "Maybe it's best you don't have the details."

"I doubt that very much."

"At least you have the comfort of eventually joining the society and having the chance of wreaking havoc to your heart's content."

"I suppose," she replied quietly. "Not that I'm one to be interested in creating mayhem."

He squeezed her hand and knew that was as far from the truth as possible because that's exactly what she'd been doing from the moment they met. And he hoped she didn't see a need to stop anytime soon since Olivia's chaos was exactly the thing he didn't know he needed.

\*\*\*

Olivia waved to Zane and then walked into her Mother's store. "Hi, Mom."

"Hello, Livy." She gave her daughter a side hug. "Why didn't Zane come in?"

"He's got to run down to the hardware store and pick up a special order he put in last week." She dropped her tote on the counter. "Zane won't admit it, but I know he and Allen have become friends, and their bi-weekly visits have little to do with paint and wrenches."

"One can never have too many friends." Elaine took Olivia's hand. "Come and keep me company while I wrap up the tofu brownies I just made."

"Alright," she followed her mother through the store and slid into a pink chair at the lunch counter. She watched her cut the delicious treats into squares with a plastic knife. "Still don't know why using plastic makes the cuts so neat and clean."

"Plastic is the ultimate non-stick surface. Bad for our planet, but excellent for not tearing up brownies."

"So…Mom…"

"If you're going to bring up Gram's ridiculous plan, please don't." She slipped a brownie into a wax bag and then tied it with a red ribbon. "The sheriff and I are friends and don't want to make it more."

"I wasn't going to, but it's nice to know that all of our careful plans were for naught."

"I think the word machinations is more fitting, but that's just me."

"Are you not interested in Mitch because you don't find him attractive or because you think Dad was your only love?"

Elaine turned. "I think people get more than one shot at love." She walked around the counter and sat. "I know what you and Thad had was special. But he was your first love, not your only one." She cupped her daughter's cheek. "I hope you have at least a half a dozen life-changing entanglements before you leave this earth."

"Are you channeling Grams?"

"Perhaps a little. Just remember that love comes in all forms, and being open to whatever comes along will make your life richer."

"Any chance of you embracing that sentiment and taking on our handsome sheriff, once and for all?"

"It takes a lot to risk your heart once you know how devastating it is to have it broken. And neither Mitch nor I am ready to endanger our friendship."

"But someday that could change, right?"

"Anything is possible."

The door creaked open, and Bea walked in with her brother, Jordan. "Hey, ladies, I'm delivering your number one stock boy five minutes early."

Olivia smiled at Mitch's kids and watched Jordan slide off his headphones. "Not interested in hearing the world today?"

"Too loud," Jordan replied.

Elaine pushed herself up and took the teenager's hand. "Would you like to work in the back today and unpack the new shipment, then?"

"Yes. I'm better at stocking the shelves than you are."

"I can't disagree," Elaine smiled and headed toward the stockroom.

"Being on the spectrum has its advantages because you can say what you think, and nobody expects you to wrap it up in some polite, socially acceptable package," Bea stated with envy.

"Is your namaste slipping today, friend?"

"A little."

"Want to talk about it?"

"Not really. Just feeling a little bruised by the world."

"I was just talking to my mom about the possibility of taking on your dad and got a big *wait and see,* which is very disappointing."

"Neither of them is ready, so leaving them be might be the best choice."

"I guess." She took her friend's hand. "Do you want to come over tonight for movies and wine?"

"I can't but would love to take a raincheck. Dad is out of town, so I've got Jordan for the next couple of days."

"You know that he's always welcome. I have all his Star Wars DVDs in the cupboard and can make him a gluten-free pizza."

Bea squeezed Olivia's hand. "That sounds lovely, but the chance of him changing his schedule is slim to none."

"I figured as much but wanted to put it out there."

She looked around the store. "Where's Zane?"

"Doing errands."

"I saw you two walking hand in hand earlier and loved seeing you with such a happy smile." She made a heart shape with her hands. "I think Zane is going to surprise you because every time he's in your company, his blue aura gets all dreamy purple. And your yellow aura gets replaced with a red juicy one.

Olivia leaned against the counter. "He's been saying the most extraordinary things, and I'm afraid if I start believing half of them, then he'll not only be delivering a ton of physical pleasure but a soulgasim."

"Whoa." Bea straightened a stack of tarot cards. "That's not what I thought you'd say."

"It's not surprising," she swept her hair off her face, "Who wouldn't be a ball of red fire if they were within a foot of the man? I doubt there's a woman alive who wouldn't feel the same way."

"I don't."

TRUST

Olivia smirked. "How could you since you and his pretty-boy brother are like two dogs circling each other deciding whether to fornicate or fight?"

Bea accidentally knocked over the stack of cards. "That's so not true."

"It sure is if what I saw at the fair is any indication." She narrowed her eyes. "Does the departure of a certain JAG officer have anything to do with your current state?"

"That's silly." Bea bent down and picked up the cards. "An unenlightened man could never have that kind of power. It's positively unimaginable."

"Mmmhmmm."

"Whatever. We're not talking about me."

"But we could."

"No, thanks." Bea strolled around the table and fixed the display. "I'd rather forget the man exists and maintain my illusion that I'm fully in charge of my destiny, and someone who resembles Apollo could never upset my chi."

"Going for the Greek god metaphor so early?"

"I was merely pointing out that Asher physically resembles the aforementioned deity." Bea let out an exasperated groan. "But in no way possesses an ounce of his lyrical charisma because the man knows nothing about poetry, light, *or* music. He's the most literal human I've ever encountered. And not in a good way."

"We are so digging into this." Olivia clapped her hands. "I've clearly missed the opening act to what is certain to be a delicious, if somewhat ill-fated, lusty affair."

Bea closed her eyes. "I will buy you all the chips your heart desires if you promise to drop the subject for the time being."

Olivia looked over her shoulder to make sure her mom was still in the back. "Are we talking white cheddar jalapeno Cheetos?"

"Yes! And I promise not to rat you out to Elaine."

"Deal, but only because I adore you and can see that you're suffering."

"It's so unsettling, Liv."

"Seems that's what the Hawker men specialize in."

Bea smoothed out her hair. "Enough about that, give me an update on the latest with you and lover boy."

"Unfortunately, I seem to be connecting with Zane more than just physically. Which isn't the good news you'd imagine since it's got my well-developed instinct for self-preservation ringing the alarm bell."

"Unless you have a black heart, it's kinda hard not to," Bea replied. "No matter what anyone says, sex means something. If only because you're exchanging energy with another human."

"I suppose so." Olivia studied a stack of satsuma oranges and tried to determine how Zane was doing the unimaginable and pressing his hands through the surface of her soul. Did he even mean to?

"There's something that needs to be worked out between the two of you," Bea said firmly. "I'm not getting a clear signal of how it's all going to turn out. But it's not something that can be avoided."

"I know," she replied, shoulders slumping.

Margret whacked open the screen and held tightly to a small white furball. "Good Lawd, why do I get myself into these things?"

"Dog napping?" Olivia asked as she squatted, watching the dog that resembled a floor mop skitter in her direction.

"As if I could fit that into my schedule," Margret sniffed. "I have agreed to help my friend find a home for this scoundrel."

Bea patted the dog. "He's too sweet to be any such thing."

"Tell that to my favorite gold sandals." She swished her hand over the small dog. "Meet Killer, ladies."

"Love the studded collar, very fitting," Olivia commented as she lifted the dog into her arms.

"What were you two talking about?" Margret asked. "The way your heads were tilted suggests it was something intriguing,"

"The feeling," Olivia said flatly.

"Oh," Grams replied, collapsing into a chair. "Which one? *Hitomebore*?"

"Not love at first sight, Grams. *Koi No Yokan*."

"What are you two talking about?" Bea asked.

"*Koi No Yokan* is a Japanese phrase that roughly translates into a premonition of love," Margret answered.

Olivia stroked Killer's soft fur. "It's that feeling you get when you meet someone and intuitively know that you could fall in love with them. You don't right now, but you *could*." Which is exactly how she'd describe the sensation that washed over her when she stood on Zane's doorstep. Which wasn't great news all around, given both of their penchants to take two steps back for every one they took forward.

"So very dangerous," Margret murmured.

Olivia took her grandmother's hand. "And who was it that made you feel that way?"

Margret lifted her strand of pearls and twisted them into a knot. "A man who was by all accounts unremarkable. But so very extraordinary in the way he made me feel." She lifted her gaze. "The way he reached for my hand and linked our fingers meant more to me than a hundred more significant gestures. We only spent a month in one another's company, but my goodness, it felt like a lifetime." She let out a little laugh. "It taught me never to underestimate the power of the wrong man. Society, your family, and even your own notions about what you deserve can steer you wrong. Pay attention, girls, to the people that light your soul on fire. Those are the ones you want to hold onto."

Olivia petted the dog. "Do I have to?"

Margret gave both women a stern look. "Absolutely! Every time you hold back the truth, you make fear more important than love."

"Which is allegedly not a good idea," Bea remarked. "Despite recent experiences suggesting otherwise."

"Isn't that the darn truth," Oliva sighed. "Does this mean I have to dig into some previously undiscovered well of bravery and run at Zane with my hair on fire?"

"A less dramatic approach could also suffice," Margret answered with an arched eyebrow.

Olivia looked out the window and caught sight of Zane talking with Allen and his daughter Zelda. "Guess it's time to go all in."

"Indeed," Grams said quietly. "And if you could take Killer when you do, that would be lovely."

"Why not?" she replied, looking down at the dog. "What's one more witness to my impending conflagration?"

## CHAPTER FIFTEEN

It was midweek, and Zane was ready to unveil his latest effort despite the unfamiliar unease filling his chest. He'd been around the world more than once, faced more foes than he could shake a stick at, and had never shrunk from any situation, no matter the odds.

That is until he met Olivia. Were his jumpy nerves due to a simple case of not wanting to disappoint the woman?

It seemed possible since giving her something she wanted had somehow become incredibly important. He heard footsteps and looked up, seeing her head in his direction. "You ready?"

She took his outstretched hand. "As I'll ever be." Looking up at the ride, she let out a happy sigh. "I've been the architect of my happiness for quite some time, so it's weird having someone who wants to…"

"Be your builder?" he finished.

"Yes."

"Well, before you make a list of things you want to do to me…I mean for me, let's see if it works."

Olivia bit her bottom lip. "Don't you worry; all efforts will be appropriately rewarded."

"I look forward to it." He gave her a confident nod and then flipped the switch on the Ferris wheel. The engine slowly rumbled to life, and he pulled her away. The old ride began moving as the rusty sound of the wheel turning filled the air. He'd taken off the passenger gondolas earlier and was glad their clanking back and forth was not part of the debut. The ride made its first revolution, and he let out a cautious breath, praying it could make a second.

Olivia let out a whoop. "You did it, Zane. Holy moly, you really can do anything."

A sense of accomplishment overwhelmed him. It turns out making another human happy was damn powerful medicine for a battered soul, after all. Lifting Olivia into his arms, he held her tightly. "Just the beginning, babe." Of what specifically, he couldn't say. But dammit, he wanted a couple more chances at being the one who made her smile.

He looked up as the wheel slowly made a second revolution. "This is a good start."

"Forget good; this is freaking amazing." She slid down his frame. "We could have this ready for the upcoming lake run and wow the town."

"The what?"

"Every year, a group of near maniacal fitness weirdos runs around the lake. People sponsor the freaks of nature, and, the more laps completed, the more money earned. All the proceeds are used for the daycare programs at the elementary schools, which is obviously a win for everyone involved."

"And how does our poor old ride figure in all that nonsense?"

Olivia slapped his chest. "Sir, where are your capitalist tendencies?"

"Not sure that I possess any since I've worked for chicken feed for longer than I care to admit." He watched her eyes narrow. "Have an opinion about that?"

"My goodness, of course, I do. How can a warrior not be paid top dollar?"

"Welcome to Spec Ops, babe. It's not a money-making gig."

"That is horrific *and* a tragedy."

"Not really." He reluctantly stepped away from her touch and flipped the switch, hearing a sound he didn't care for. "I did get to live out every dream of glory and honor, after all."

Olivia pursed her lips. "Well, I suppose there isn't a price tag you can put on something like that."

"Exactly."

"Anyway, we need to bilk our generous townsfolk out of their spare change and charge for a ride on," she waved her hand, "this beauty."

Zane ran his hand over his neck. "Exactly how long do we have before this happens?"

"Two weeks."

He glanced at the passenger gondolas. "Lots to accomplish."

"Together, it's completely doable." She lifted herself and kissed him soundly. "We'll have to cut down on our dirty afternoon escapades, but it's worth it."

He shifted his hips and liked the resulting smile. "You sure that's something we're capable of?"

"Yes," she said on a groan. "We'll just double down in the evening."

"I like the way you think, woman."

Olivia stepped back and retied her bow. "Of course, you do. Since so much of what I spend my time deliberating about is what I'd like to try next." She grabbed his hand. "All I ask is that you don't make me a fool."

"How did we go from sexy escapades to me screwing up so quickly?"

She flapped her hands. "I'm putting it out there, just in case."

"Believe it or not, I'm trying my best. I want you happy, not pissed off and planning my demise."

"I know that you believe that, but at some point, you may decide that your earlier assessment was accurate."

Not liking the turn the conversation had taken, he moved closer. "Meaning?"

"Your hermitty life may ultimately prove to be more alluring than taking me on. Hanging out with someone isn't always easy. There are…the inevitable misunderstandings and hurt feelings."

"You think I'm gonna spook again, don't you? Leave you vulnerable?"

Looking down at the ground, she let out a sigh. "It's possible."

He lifted her chin and flinched when he saw uncertainty swimming in her beautiful eyes. He'd put that there, dammit. "I'm not promising some kind of happy ever after, but I will try." He closed his eyes and let his mouth drop to hers. "With everything I've got."

"Oh, Zane." She pressed their mouths together. "I want nothing more than to roll around in the mind-blowing things you've been saying. Really allow myself to marinate in the heart-felt loveliness. But I'm desperately afraid if I do let my guard down, you won't be interested anymore. Once you've got me, you may not want to hold on."

"I can't make guarantees but will do my best to navigate these unfamiliar waters without capsizing our little boat."

"I can't ask for more." She fisted her hand into his shirt. "But if you do have a change of heart, tell me first. Don't string me along and make me guess. I'll accept your truth but won't tolerate your ambiguity."

"Fair enough."

"Because if you decide that you've had enough and then do some sort of poorly thought-out imitation of a ghost and disappear without explanation, I will not hesitate to call upon the Haven Ladies' Society to make things right."

He bent down so their faces were close. "Duly noted. And for the record, I have no desire to be on the wrong side of those women."

"What about my sides? Aren't you worried about me?"

"Of course. I'm not a damn fool."

"And Zane…"

"Yeah, Liv?"

"You've made an ordinary day extraordinary. You beautiful man."

Gobsmacked. He coughed, hoping it would clear the emotion clogging his throat. "I don't know about that."

"It's clear that you're uncomfortable with my proclamations, but too bad." Taking his hand, she swung it back and forth. "Eventually, my emotional freewheeling won't even make you blink."

"I doubt it."

Olivia cupped his scarred cheek. "Said without an ounce of conviction."

"Leave me be, woman."

"For now." She spun around and pointed at the gondolas. "I'm thinking pink."

"Of course, you are."

"My sister, Callie, would say it's totally on brand, so how could I not?"

"Not sure what that means?"

"Pink is more than just one of my aura colors; it's also my signature."

"That I get." He gave her a wink and knew his signature gray was soon going to change since a small slice of optimism was taking up permanent residence next to the pain and guilt that had made a home in his chest.

A damn miracle, as far as he could tell.

\*\*\*

Olivia sat on her midnight blue couch and studied what she could only assume was a dog standoff. Grams had dropped Killer off earlier, and Bella was deeply underwhelmed—and slightly miffed, if she wasn't mistaken.

So much for one big, happy family.

There was a light knock, and she stood, seeing Betsy Yarlin standing on the other side of the screen. "Come in, neighbor."

"Sorry to stop by without calling."

"Since when do we stand on formalities?" She pushed open the screen door and welcomed her neighbor inside.

Betsy held up a small canvas bag. "I ran into your sister, and she said you'd be interested in any spells that worked."

She accepted the bag and peeked inside. "You're loaning me all of these?"

"Giving," Betsy clarified. "Hoyt Doherty is no longer of interest, and I will not waste another minute mooning over that infuriating man!"

Olivia checked her watch and then grabbed Betsy's hand. "We're taking this conversation into the kitchen. It's just about five, and that kind of declaration needs to be accompanied by some alcohol."

"I won't disagree since I've finally admitted to myself that I've wasted years thinking that Hoyt was shy and just needed time." She collapsed into a chair at the small kitchen table. "The sad truth is, he never saw me as anything more than a friend."

Olivia quickly made two gin and tonics and plunked them on the table, along with a bowl of almonds. "Did he say that specifically, or was it something you inferred from his behavior?"

"I asked him point-blank if he ever thought about kissing me, and he got so flustered that he all but ran away." She lifted the drink and took a big gulp. "I've never seen a six-foot-five man move so quickly. You would've thought I asked him if he'd like to run down Main Street naked." Swiping her blonde hair back, she let out a sigh. "Which means casting a spell on his sorry behind would just be a waste of my love juju, and I can't be doing that anymore."

Olivia clinked her glass against Betsy's. "Amen."

Betsy sat forward and frowned. "What are those dogs doing?"

She glanced over her shoulder. "Having a standoff. Grams foisted Killer on me, and Bella is having none of it."

"Why don't you take the dog over to the Hawker homestead and let the spirits decide if he'd be a good match for Zane."

"I was thinking about sharing my dog bounty with him but wasn't sure he'd appreciate the gesture since he thinks that being a recluse is still an option."

"Wait, weren't you two kissing in front of your mom's store the other day?"

"Yes, but having sexual chemistry with someone doesn't mean long-term potential exists."

"So true. But at this point, I'd be more than happy with an actual date that was mildly entertaining."

Olivia frowned. "Don't you settle, Betsy. Just because one fellow doesn't see your magic doesn't mean a dozen others won't." She took a sip of her drink. "I bet a bunch of men in town will be elated to know that you're available. Most probably assumed that your friendship with Hoyt was a precursor to something permanent. We need to get the word out that you're single and ready to mingle."

"I guess that's exactly what I am." She tapped her nails on the table. "Maybe I should get a makeover before we make any sort of announcement, though."

"I don't think that's necessary, but maybe a new haircut that makes you feel sassy wouldn't be a bad idea. Channel your inner Lizzo and let your juice shine." She watched her quiet friend sit up and square her shoulders. "There are too many ordinary things in life; don't let your love life be one of them."

Betsy pushed herself to her feet. "You are right. It's past time I got started on a new chapter." She hugged Olivia and then headed to the door. "Thanks for the pep talk."

"Anytime." Olivia finished her drink and noticed that Killer had lost interest in the doggy showdown and was headed her way. The little darling dropped at her feet, and she patted his head. "Keep that move handy when I introduce you to your new dog-dad." She received a short bark and nodded. "And don't be put off by Zane's steel façade and general grumpiness. Because I'm almost one hundred percent confident that beneath all that bluster lies a big squishy heart."

At least that's what her slightly dented heart was hoping because she was just about ready to give in and start believing in every heartfelt sentiment he'd thrown her way.

Which meant that her excuses about keeping herself protected were going to fall apart faster than her fitness plans. Shivering at the possibility, she put it out of her mind and started concocting a scheme to get Killer and Zane smitten with one another.

Olivia sat on Zane's front stoop and held her breath. Killer was playing to his audience beautifully, and the contented sighs coming out of the tiny beast didn't seem in the least bit nefarious. The white ball of fluff was keen on Zane, and there wasn't an ounce of fakery involved.

"You said a month, right?"

"At the most." She crossed her fingers behind her back, praying the white lie wouldn't come back to bite.

"I guess it would be okay." He ran his hand over the dog's back. "He can run around without much chance of getting hurt."

"I doubt he's going to want to leave your side."
The dog was curled into Zane's lap, and she knew any
attempt to move him would likely be meant with a
good bit of sharp teeth. "Maybe you can teach him a
few things while you're together."

"The first being that's he's overplaying his
audience?" Zane asked as Killer whined and scrabbled
closer. "The dog has got your sense of the dramatic.
Are you sure Bella wouldn't eventually welcome him
into the pack?"

"She's made her opinion on the matter clear, and
I'm not ready to test how vehemently she might
defend her turf." Ignoring Zane's impressive side-eye,
she studied the trees.

"You know I'm not buying any of this, right?"

She whipped her head around. "Whatever are
you talking about?"

"You think I need a dog because of the way Bella
helped me with one of my episodes." He shook his
head. "Babe, I can spot someone on my six a mile
out. I know you saw me pulled into an old memory
yesterday and took note of how Bella stayed at my
side until I could drag myself back into the present."

Biting her bottom lip, she stroked Killer's soft
fur. "Are you mad?"

"Not really." He covered her hand. "But ignoring
stuff probably isn't good."

She ran her finger over a scar that bisected his
knuckles. "I didn't want you to feel more self-
conscious than you already do." She ran her eyes over
his face. "Though how you would still feel any
trepidation about me or the folks in town is a
mystery. Women want to know you, and men want to
become your friend."

"I don't know if that's true."

"Whatever." She leaned into his shoulder. "Do you like Killer?"

"His name should be lover boy." He lifted the dog off his lap and set him on the ground. "And yes, I think he's fine."

"A ringing endorsement."

"That's about as enthusiastic as I'm gonna get over this little dust mop." He dropped his arm over Olivia's shoulder. "And please don't take this one exception as a sign that I need any more wayward animals."

"Of course."

He smirked. "I know that you're not being sincere. How can you be both infuriating and irresistible?"

She scooted closer and ran her hand over his mouth. "It's a gift."

"I'm starting to understand that."

"Can I assume the sparks in your eyes are of a sexual nature?"

Zane cupped her face and pressed their mouths together. "You can pretty much count on it."

"Lucky me," she mumbled against his mouth. She gave him a dirty kiss and was relishing his response when the sound of a loud motorcycle engine bounced against the trees.

Zane pulled away and stood. "What the hell?"

Olivia joined him and heard Killer let out some impressive sharp barks. "A family member?"

Zane descended the steps and let out a laugh when a large man parked the bike and slid off his helmet. "Cousin Linc? What the hell are you doing here?"

"Heard you were trying to tame the family ghosts alone." He ran his hand through his hair and looked up at the three-story structure. "Figured I'd come and help."

Olivia watched a rare open smile form on Zane's face and knew that another Hawker in residence wasn't going to be a bad thing.

And not just because the man was too handsome for words. She lifted Killer into her arms and gave herself a moment to consider what kind of genetic lottery produced so many good looking, magnetic men.

Certainly, any progeny they produced would be equally as lucky. Not that she was thinking about what kind of munchkins she and Zane could create.

How ridiculous.

\*\*\*

Zane waved to Olivia and then walked back into his house with the new dog on his heels. "Where you at, cousin?"

Linc descended the stairs. "Family gossip suggested you were going with a recluse thing." He planted his feet at the bottom of the stairs and crossed his arms. "But I have to call bullshit because you've got a charming girlfriend and a dog that won't leave your side."

"If I told you this wasn't my plan, would you believe me?"

"Of course, since good fortune is pure serendipity." He lifted his arm and checked his watch. "Do we have time for a beer before we're expected at Chateau Bennett for supper?"

"Absolutely." He slapped his cousin on the shoulder and acknowledged that he was glad for the company. Another fact he could pile on top of all the others that told him his plan for solitude had more holes than a piece of swiss cheese.

Once they were settled with beers, Zane studied his cousin. "I never heard how your departure from the Navy went."

"A hell of a lot better than Asher's if gossip is to be believed." He lifted the bottle to his mouth and took a gulp. "A decade as a boat guy was everything I could've hoped for. High risk, high adventure. Lots of good done."

"I heard you pulled Colt's team out of a dicey situation a couple of times."

"Sure did." He threw Zane a wink. "Not that I'm talking about it, though."

"The baby of the family is always the most talkative and the one with the least fear."

"Ain't that the truth." He shook his head. "Worry not; your brother has found his home on the Teams and is making a name for himself, just like Rorke did."

"Wouldn't expect less."

"And how's your transition going?"

Zane drained his beer. "Not as much of a catastrophe as you'd expect."

"Guessing that pretty lady from the down the lane is helping."

"Not sure about that." He ran his hand over his neck. "It sure is testing me, though."

"As all good things do." Linc tipped back in his chair. "God isn't going to give you the good stuff unless he or she is sure you can handle it."

"For the record, war is a hell of a lot easier than love. And anyone who tells you differently is full of shit."

"The fact you used the L-word pretty much answers my next question."

"I was speaking metaphorically."

"You don't have a figurative bone in your whole damn body, but I'm not gonna bust your chops too much. You go on and enjoy the fantasy that Olivia is just a distraction." Linc shook his head. "But when you're done rolling around in your own bullshit, know that if you want a lover, then you gotta be a fighter."

"What the hell are you talking about?"

"Fight to do the right thing. In life, love, and the pursuit of whatever is formidable. Including vanquishing those memories you like to lug around." Linc smirked. "If you're in hell right now—swing! Channel that heartache, soul-ache, and whatever other kinds of ache you got and fight for the right thing." He tipped his chin. "You won't forgive yourself otherwise. Don't start bowing now."

Zane plunked his empty bottle down. "And what made you think I was kneeling to anything?"

"Those heavy shoulders you got."

The small dog in his lap whined, and he decided that God was bringing in the heavy guns. He hadn't spent a day in his cousin's company in years. Yet here he was laying down the truth like a damn preacher. And it wasn't because Linc was prone to give people advice—because he wasn't. The man lived hard, played hard, and rode odds that never should've worked out for…anyone. He lived by his own code and counsel and expected others to do the same.

"You ever consider that what you're feeling has been well earned?"

"Happiness?" Zane asked.

"Yeah!"

"Didn't think I deserved something like that." He rubbed his finger over the bottle in his hand.

"That's about the dumbest thing I've heard you say because you have paid the piper and are due for some righteous blessings." He shook his head. "The battlefield is where peace is won. Joy is on the other side of a skirmish. Conflict isn't the opposite of joy; it's the path to it. The road in."

"But…"

"Instead of calculating how many lives you didn't bring home, count the ones you did."

"Damn, when the hell did you become so freaking Zen? Did you sneak off to an ashram when you were stationed in San Diego?"

"Don't knock my mental health, man. It was a long-fought battle, and not one step of it was easy." Linc pushed himself out of the chair. "So, tell me about your girl. Does she have any pretty sisters or friends?"

Head spinning at the turn of the conversation, Zane leaned back. "She's got both. Her older sister owns the bookstore in town, and her best friend has a yoga studio. She's got a younger sister that I haven't met and about a hundred friends that I can't keep straight."

"I saw a pretty redhead in front of the bookstore on my way in. Is that a Bennett sister?"

"Yep. That's Lucy, the town heart breaker as far as I can tell."

"She can break something on me." Linc pulled two beers out of the fridge and returned to the table. "That woman is temptation. Pure and simple." He flipped the caps off and sat down. "A goddamn piece of dark chocolate cake that no one can resist."

Zane crossed his arms. "That's a lot more adjectives than one pass should've provided."

"I might've stopped and taken a moment to enjoy the scenery."

"Okay." He studied his cousin and couldn't tell if there was more. Or if he wanted to know about it. Not that Lucy Bennett couldn't handle Linc Hawker, legendary Lothario. Because she surely could. The little time they'd spent in one another's company told him there wasn't a man or invasion of a small country she couldn't manage with little effort—in a dress, high heels, and some damn sparkly jewelry, to boot. He shook his head and decided those were facts his cousin could discover on his own.

His hands were full as it was. He had a tiger by the tail and didn't have an ounce of confidence that he'd come out the victor. Not that he wanted there to be a losing side when it came to Olivia and him. He just didn't want to be worse off than he was. Killer licked his hand and then tilted his head. "Don't overplay your hand, dog. I'm already keeping you."

"You ever think giving in and raising the white flag is more expeditious?"

"To total ruin?" Zane asked.

"Or happiness," Linc replied quietly.

"A lot more than I'm comfortable admitting."

"Yeah, man, same."

Zane slid his finger over the condensation on the cold beer bottle and told himself that giving in wasn't giving up. It was just a road he wasn't all that familiar with.

How perilous could the road less traveled be anyway?

## CHAPTER SIXTEEN

Olivia looked around at her guests and tried to pinpoint the moment when the cocktail hour had gone off the rails. She lifted her wine glass and drained it, deciding the wine had nothing to do with it. Nor did the pimiento cheese and crackers since they were delicious as always.

And what for the love of God was happening between her sister and Zane's cousin? The tension that ignited the moment they'd been introduced was making her light-headed.

Was unwanted lust responsible? It seemed possible since her sister was almost immediately out of sorts—a rare occurrence in a man's company or anyone's for that matter. Lucy could easily carry on civil discourse with even the most objectional human. And Linc certainly wasn't that since he was handsome as sin with a delightful rakish wit.

The two were currently nose-to-nose and speaking in heated whispers.

Then there were Bea and Asher pretending like the other didn't exist. They were both studying the walls with a lot more interest than the art deserved and refilling their wine glasses at an alarming rate. She'd tried every conversational trick she could think of, and none of them had worked.

When they showed up together, unannounced and unexpected, she knew something had gone down. Asher's sudden appearance in town had flummoxed her best friend, and whatever happened before they arrived was clearly of consequence. And she'd bet good money it was some kind of lip-lock that had them acting like they'd prefer to be in a Russian gulag instead of her lovely dinner party.

And then there was her Zane; he too looked like he wanted to be anywhere else. The sound of Linc's and Lucy's heated whispers increased, and she sighed. "What do you suppose is going on? I can't tell if they're flirting or fussing."

Zane thrummed his fingers restlessly on his knee. "No idea, Liv. Maybe we should just call it and forget dinner."

She tamped down her frustration. He'd been strung tight since he arrived, and she didn't know if the domesticity of the evening had him on edge or something else completely. Did he think that having dinner *en famille* meant that she was interested in some sort of formal arrangement? Because she most certainly wasn't.

Her life was full, with nary a free moment for a consuming relationship. Naughty shenanigans, yes. Formal relationship, probably not. Her matrimonial death glare was packed safely away, and she had no plans to dig it out any time soon.

Tired of her mental machinations, she pushed herself to her feet. "I'm going to check on supper."

"I'll help," Zane added loudly.

Nothing. There was no reaction from Linc and Lucy or Asher and Bea. All four of them were engaged in some kind of weird quiet exchange of silent stinging looks. Sighing, she tromped into the kitchen and pulled open the oven door, checking on the roasted chicken she was planning to serve. That was if anyone decided to hang around for dinner.

"My dinner parties don't usually start so badly."

Zane refilled her wine glass and then pulled out another beer. "This is why entertaining is a bad idea."

She turned a burner on and slid over a pot filled with potatoes. "Having people over is not ill-advised. Clearly, there's some kind of boy-girl drama happening, and I bet by the time we sit down to this delicious meal, detente will have been achieved."

Zane snorted. "Not likely."

Narrowing her eyes, she shook some salt into the pan. "Feel like sharing what's got you wound tighter than a clock?" She waved a wooden spoon in the direction of the porch. "It can't be the company since two belong to your family."

"They're your guests, Liv. Not ours."

"Ooohhhh," she said quietly. "I get it."

"What the hell does that mean?"

*Here we go*, she thought as she lifted her wine glass. "Nothing, Zane."

"The condescension in the comment tells me it's goddamn something."

Frustrated beyond measure, she set her glass down and spun around. "You want to fight with someone, go to the other room and choose one of your relatives." She picked up the spoon. "All I did was invite you and your cousin over for dinner. It's not a sign that I'm interested in some sort of domesticity together." Slapping the spoon down on the counter, she let out a groan. "As surprising as it might be, your ever-present cloud of doom and gloom isn't all that attractive." She waved her hands. "I don't have you handcuffed to my side, so go home and glower at your dead relatives."

"Jeez, I'm sorry." Zane kicked the ground. "It's just…"

"That you saw a glimpse of what we could be and freaked out. Did pissing me off seem easier than just admitting you're not ready for anything serious?" She resisted his hand tugging hers for a couple of seconds and then gave in. He pulled her into his chest, and she wished that it didn't feel so damn much like home.

"I've been fighting an anxiety attack since I got here, and…"

"It's not going well," she whispered.

"Nope."

"And starting a fight seemed like a good answer?"

"Believe it or not, that wasn't what I was trying to do." He skated his hand along her back. "I have no idea how to deal with this crap. I'm accustomed to dominating every space I enter."

"You may need some new ammo for your current enemy because your emotions don't likely have a whole lot of respect for bullets or bombs."

"Yeah, I know."

"Feel like doing anything about developing some new skills, so the dragons circling your castle begin to respect your majesty?"

"Believe it or not, I do."

She pushed at his chest and stepped back. "I'm not asking for me; it's for you, Zane." She lifted her hand and ran it over his grim smile. "You are a good person and have more than paid the price for whatever you think you did or didn't do."

He let out a resigned grunt. "Does that mean we can stay in the kitchen and eat supper in peace?"

"And miss the show our friends and family are putting on? No way!"

"It's so damn uncomfortable, though."

She patted his chest. "If I may be so bold, I'd like to offer another perspective."

Zane rolled his hand. "Go ahead, babe, because we both know I'm powerless in refusing you."

Pursing her lips, she smoothed out his shirt. "As it should be." She saw her sister in the doorway. "More drinks?"

"I'm...going home. Headache."

"I'm taking her," Linc announced loudly from behind.

"I can..." Before she could finish her sentence, they both strode toward the door. "Well, that's unfortunate." She walked out to the porch and found it empty. "We've been abandoned, Zane."

"What the hell?" he asked as he joined her. "Where did Asher and Bea go?"

"Do they have something against roast chicken and mashed potatoes?"

Zane slung his arm over Olivia's shoulder. "What were you saying about another perspective?"

"Never mind," she huffed. "If they want to deny us a front-row seat to the opening scene of what is clearly a very good show, then so be it."

"Does this mean we can eat in the kitchen and feel each other up?"

She let her shoulders drop. "Might as well since my dinner party is a disaster." Lifting her gaze, she exhaled. "Why are you enjoying this?"

He put up his hands. "I'm not. But damn if I'm not going to revel in the fact that my behavior wasn't the worst of the evening." Taking her hand, he lifted it to his mouth and kissed her fingers. "I thought my anxiety was going be center stage, but instead, it's my family's bad manners."

"And mine." She headed back into the kitchen and hoped that Zane would eventually put some time and effort into his mental health. And not just because she wanted him eventually to enjoy her social efforts. But because he was too good a man not to appreciate the beautiful moments when they came along.

## CHAPTER SEVENTEEN

Zane gave a short knock and then walked through Olivia's screen door. There was a plate of brownies on the counter, and he wondered who they were intended for. In their short acquaintance, he'd discovered that her efforts in the kitchen were usually on someone else's behalf.

Salt was her go-to, and she could crush a bag of chips faster than he thought possible. "Liv, it's me."

"Who goes there?"

"How many me's you got banging through your door?"

"So, so many," she replied with laughter as she walked into the kitchen. "Whatcha doing here, Zane?"

She sauntered over and slid her hands up his T-shirt, making his heart beat out of rhythm. "I came to take you for a walk around the lake. Maybe a swim if you're up for it."

"Really?"

"I'm more than a boy toy, woman, and will not give in to your libidinous demands."

"If I give you that pan of brownies, will you reconsider?"

"If you go for a walk, I might." She slipped her hands away from his chest, and he wondered why he was such a dumb ass and not giving them both what they were hungry for. Shaking off the weak moment, he arched an eyebrow.

"Fine, but only because it's impossible to ignore your use of a fifteen-point word." She ran her hand over his forearm. "Libidinous indeed."

"I'll wait outside." He spun around and pushed through the door, knowing that he was a breath away from taking her against the wall.

Keeping half their time together clothed was no small feat, and there were many moments when he didn't know why he tried. They had more sparks than a Fourth of July firework display, and it was taking all his good intentions not to spend every waking moment rolling around naked with the too tempting woman.

He strode across the grass and then doubled-back. Then he did it again, just in case.

The slap of the screen door and Bella running at him full speed got his mind refocused, and he stopped the dog right before she plowed into his leg. "Guess you like the idea of the walk."

"She'll be searching for her one true love," Olivia called out. "Our black cat has been missing for more than a week, and my girl is a tad distressed."

He held out his hand. "Well, let's go see if we can find him." Bella barked and then took off, heading toward the woods.

Olivia held up a water bottle. "I brought hydration."

"Thanks, babe."

"Not that we'll need it since you seem dead set on behaving."

He cut across the yard and followed Bella toward the lake. "Did you always want to be a medical illustrator?"

Olivia stopped abruptly. "You are serious. About this talking thing."

He tugged on her hand. "The day we met, you made a lot of noise about wanting to know me and digging into my long-held dreams. Was that just a show?"

"Absolutely not." She walked beside him. "I've just gotten a little distracted by your," she waved her hand over his body, "other fine attributes."

"Well, you can think of this as a way to get refocused."

"Fine, but I expect you to give up some juicy info. I already know the most pertinent facts and am ready to hear your more hidden truths."

"What about you, woman? You've revealed very little, and it makes me think it's you that has a secret life."

Snorting, she squeezed his hand. "Hardly. I went to college and graduate school in Virginia and then…came home. I've barely made it out of town and have a small quiet life."

"No desire to see the world?" he asked.

"It took me a bit longer than I expected to move on from the accident, and my need to stay close to the wall, so to speak, has lasted for quite some time." She looked up. "Your arrival is the most exciting thing to happen in ages."

"Don't know how that's possible."

"What about you, Zane? Has your taste for adventure been satisfied?"

"Present company excluded?"

"I can hardly be considered an adventure."

"Babe, you're nothing short of a diamond run."

"Huh, a skiing analogy. Not sure how I feel about that."

"Considering I'm a Green Beret, it should make you just about ecstatic since I've got a taste for near-death experiences." He took the trail that led to the lake and allowed himself a moment to appreciate the sun bouncing off the water. "Does this place still take your breath away, or are you immune to it?"

"When I take the time to notice, it sure the heck does."

"Any place you want to see in this big old world?"

"Of course," Liv replied, taking his hand. "But I don't want you to laugh at my top choice."

"Why would I laugh?"

"Because it's mundane and a bit boring."

Zane stopped near the edge of the water and listened to it lap against the shore. "I'm not a man that needs impressing. Though you do, for the record. In the most unexpected ways."

"Really?"

"Yeah, Liv. Absolutely."

"Well, that's surprising."

He slung his arm over Liv's shoulders and pulled her to his side. "So, where do you want to go?"

"Hawaii."

Olivia's rested her head against his chest, and déjà vu hit him squarely in the chest—along with an unmistakable feeling of fate.

Was Olivia his future happiness? A ball of wild and untamed emotions bounced in his chest like a pinball and he knew that the answer was on the other side of his painful memories.

"I told you it was boring."

He shook himself out of his thoughts and looked into Olivia's hesitant smile. "Warm water, soft sand, you in a bikini. Yeah, that sounds awful." He embraced her tightly and let a picture of the two of them on Kauai fill his mind. "It would be nothing less than torture to swim with the dolphins and drink ridiculous tropical cocktails together. We definitely should never go."

"Yeah, who'd want to skinny dip in the moonlight?" She looked around and then wiggled out of his embrace. "We should just do it here and get it over with."

Zane let out a short chuckle. And then he watched her T-shirt fly over her head. "Liv, there's still plenty of daylight."

"Well aware of that," she said with a giggle. "Underwear and bathing suits are not that much different."

His mouth went dry. "Except one is see-through, and the other isn't."

She slid her shorts off her legs and kicked off her sandals. "Then I guess you'll have to defend my honor if a raccoon starts to gawk." Taking a step back, she gave him a naughty grin. "Come on, adventure boy, join me."

Before he could respond, she took off and jumped in with a loud whoop. Her head disappeared for a moment and then surfaced. He pulled his shirt over his head and then got rid of his shorts. He wasn't worried about some animal getting an eyeful of his woman, but a damn stranger.

He didn't share, and, despite his reservations, concerns, and overall wariness of getting too deeply involved, Liv was his. He strode down to the lake and jumped into the water, praying no one showed up.

Diving under the warm lake water, he cut the space that separated him from his naked water nymph and grabbed her ass with both hands before cresting the surface. "Gotcha."

Turning so they were face to face, Olivia rested her hands on Zane's shoulders. "Are you a friendly sea monster or one that consumes its prey under the cover of moonlight?"

He planted his feet and pulled her closer. "Depends on the day."

"Speaking of monsters, how are your beasts doing? Giving you any trouble today?"

Looking up into the endless blue sky, he gave a short shake of his head. "No, I told 'em to take the day off and stay home."

Olivia stroked his cheek and then leaned forward, bestowing the gentlest of kisses. "Might as well give them the whole month off. We've got better things to do with our time and don't need their company."

"If only it were that easy." He moved toward deeper water with Olivia anchored against his chest. "I'm never sure when the anxiety is going to hit, and, as far as I'm concerned, there's nothing worse. I'm a lot more comfortable having some kind of idea when the enemy is going to show up, and these surprise attacks are bullshit."

"I found that cognitive-behavioral therapy worked when I was dealing with them after the accident. It took a fair amount of work, but eventually, I had the upper hand more often than not."

"The head shrinker from the army said it was probably my best option. She also suggested that willing them away with my hard-headed stubbornness likely wasn't a fool-proof battle plan."

"Yeah, I might've heard something along those lines too."

He pushed wet hair off Olivia's face and was hit all over again by her incredible light and kindness. She was good medicine, and he had a feeling that if he ever completely gave in to the feelings she inspired…well, it would be damn impossible to let her go. "Appreciate you, woman."

"Really?" She leaned her face into his hand. "I feel a couple of quips trying to escape, but I'm not going to let them because this moment with you deserves better."

"It sure does." Knowing he would never find the words worthy, he let his mouth find hers. He fit their lips together and knew destiny was knocking like a son of a bitch on his door.

How long would it take him to dig up enough courage to answer?

Deciding those mental machinations could wait for another day, he focused on Olivia's passionate response to his kiss. Her small hands dug into his shoulders, and the low moans that escaped filled the air around them, igniting his need.

Ending the kiss reluctantly, he pulled her into his chest. "I think we've fulfilled the outing requirement for the day."

Laughter spilled out of Olivia, and he swam for the shore. "We can move on…"

"To the ravaging," Olivia finished as she clung to him like a monkey.

"I was gonna say sweet, sweet lovemaking, but we can go with your idea."

"Thank God."

He dropped her gently to the ground and lifted the pile of their discarded clothes. "But we're gonna have to do it at your house since mine is full of relatives."

Olivia took her clothes and stepped into her shorts. "Speaking of that, did you get any intel about exactly what went down last night and why they ditched us?"

"I got grunts as answers when I checked in with them earlier."

"That won't do."

"Men are lousy at sharing the details." He slid his T-shirt on. "What did the ladies say?"

"Nothing," Olivia whined. "They are both avoiding my calls."

"Looks like a wait-and-see situation."

Olivia snorted. "Zane, we both know that I'm not a wait-and-see kinda gal."

Shoving his feet into his shoes, he gave her a grin. "Get to it, then."

"Believe me; I will be on the case and have a bag full of facts before you know it."

"You can start right after I deliver a couple of mind-bending orgasms."

Olivia whistled for Bella and then took a couple of steps back. "Less talking Zane, more action."

The dog crashed through the trees heading toward home, and Olivia followed her. Not a man to ignore an order, he jogged in her direction and prayed he could wrangle his demons into submission before too long.

Women like Olivia didn't come along more than once in a man's life and the last thing he wanted to do was screw-up his one chance for happiness.

## CHAPTER EIGHTEEN

Oliva tossed a dress on her bed and thought about endings, wondering why the universe couldn't manage clearer signs when a crash and burn was imminent.

She was fairly certain that the brief acrimonious encounters she'd shared with Zane over the last week were meant to be just that but couldn't be certain.

The weather pattern had been unpredictable, and she didn't know if he was going to snarl or take her into his arms like it was his last day on earth when he happened to stop by.

Bella barked out a greeting as the screen door slapped shut. "Friend or foe?"

Heavy footsteps clomped against the wooden floors, and she assumed the latest Zane storm was about to land on her shores.

She sighed, lifted a dress off the pile, and prayed it would fit better than the last.

"Hey, Liv, what are you doing?"

"Hello, neighbor." She dropped the dress on the bed and tried to calculate the chances of being blessed with the mother of all *it's not you, it's me* speeches. "How have you been?"

"Not much different than when you saw me a couple of days ago." Zane looked down at the dog on his heel. "I can't seem to shake this little beast."

Stepping back, she told herself that there wasn't a bite of recrimination in his tone but one of frustration. "I guess he's enamored and showing you some proper hero worship."

"Where are you going?" He lifted a discarded dress and frowned. "We don't have special plans that I've forgotten about, right?"

She snorted and immediately saw his frown deepen. "We've yet to have a date, sir. So the answer is no, we've got no plans. Special or otherwise."

"We've been places."

"We've done errands and grabbed a sandwich, so I suppose there is some truth in that. But you've never asked me out on a proper date." His generous mouth flattened into a firm line. Was she not supposed to point that out? "So, anyway, what have you and Linc been up to?"

"You done with me already?" He dropped the dress and crossed his arms. "Did you find yourself someone new who will play the part of Prince Charming with enthusiasm?"

A cold feeling of dread slid along her spine. "Why are you starting a fight? Were you too lazy to craft a decent *see-ya* speech?" The way his body bristled with anger didn't bother her as much as she expected. It seemed she did have lines that couldn't be crossed, and her self-respect truly was alive and well.

"You didn't answer the question!"

"I don't know who peed in your Cheerios, but I will not be baited into a ridiculous skirmish." She lifted the pile of dresses. "I have all kinds of feelings for you, but this is not a day to test which ones rise to the top." She marched into her closet and counted backward from fifty, hoping she could get her temper under control by the time she rehung her clothes.

The man was beyond infuriating, and she was beginning to think that their brief moments of connection were not going to be enough. It was up to him to evict his ever-present demons. The ones that told him he didn't deserve better and the only way to balance the ledger was to sacrifice his life right alongside the men that didn't make it home.

Sayonara happy sex hormones. They were no match for the pain and loss he clung to.

Not that she thought the connection they occasionally managed would be. She wasn't a damn fool, after all.

Or was she? She straightened the hangers and decided she was as centered as she was going to get. It was time to deal with the exasperating man and then get on with her day. When she stepped out of her closet, she saw Zane standing next to the window. "I can make up a hundred stories about what has caused your behavior, or you can just tell me. There's no need to put on a big show. If you've lost interest, just say it."

Doing what she could to ignore the uncertainty in his eyes, she attempted a small fortification of her emotional walls—*not going to settle for ambiguity and not going to settle for yes one minute and no the next. Not going to settle for mind-blowing sex in exchange for...* that last thought was perhaps a bit hasty. It might be best to leave that one alone for now. "I have plenty of wine, chips, and vats of ice cream. I'm more than able to handle you scuttling off like a wounded bear and disappearing into your cave."

The gust of air that escaped his mouth was impressive, and she guessed that he found her slightly theatrical but no doubt entertaining plea slightly annoying. "I'm ready, Zane. Hit me with your best departing speech."

"I have no idea what the hell I'm doing." He stalked over and took her hand. "And I don't have some kind of speech prepared." He leaned back and studied her face. "Is that disappointment I see?"

"No," she sputtered. "Okay, maybe a little since I have two snappy comebacks and one mind-bending retort ready."

"I'm sorry that I've been acting like an ass. I know how to be a warrior on the front lines." He twisted his mouth. "It's probably the place I'm most comfortable. And truth be told, there are days when I want nothing more than to be back in the fight. Because there's nothing like the rush of adrenaline when you have a chance to take out the enemy, whoever it might be."

She ran her finger over a puckered scar on his forearm and assumed it was from a bullet. "Right now, I'm the only enemy you've got since I've messed with your hermit plans. I'm the disrupter in the quiet life you were hoping to find."

"You're not…"

She held her breath, letting it out slowly when he didn't say more. "I'm going to kick you out so I can get ready."

"What kind of plans require you to show off those damn fine legs of yours?" He moved closer. "Do I have to take up my sword and show the competition what they have to look forward to?"

"As if you'd do such a thing." Feeling his grip tighten, she looked up. "All your recent bluster and bad manners suggest you'd like nothing more than to be free of my attention."

"Not free, Liv."

"Not really buying that, but no matter."

"Do you need a ride to wherever you're going?"

"No, Zane. It's the sixth anniversary of Thad's passing, and I'm having dinner with his brother and best friend."

"Ah, jeez. I'm sorry."

"No problem." She turned toward her bathroom. "You can bring Killer over in the morning. No need to try and make it work."

"It's fine. He's not bad and can stay at the house."

"Dogs and people deserve a lot more than fine." Not wanting to drag the conversation on longer, she stepped away. "You take care, Zane." She walked into her bathroom and closed the door. "Some stories are not meant to be written, and there's no changing that." She flipped on the water and then stared at her reflection in the mirror. "Hard days don't last forever. Take one step and then another until you're in a place that feels okay."

She dropped her head as the small room filled with steam, reminding herself that she'd already had the worst day of her life. Feeling a smidge better, she stepped into the shower and was grateful that she'd kept her soft heart somewhat protected. Zane's ambivalence was stronger than his desire, and that was a fact she'd do well to keep front of mind.

\*\*\*

Zane sat back on his knees and accepted that he was welcomed by the inhabitants of Haven. No one gave him a wide berth, whispered behind his back, or made him feel unwanted in any way. In fact, several of them were populating Olivia's yard as they helped him and Linc finish the rehab on the Ferris wheel.

Allen lumbered in his direction, and he pushed himself to his feet. "You heading out?"

"No, I've got myself a hall pass and the evening to do with as I please."

"Get out of here then and do something fun."

Allen tipped his chin in the direction of the gondolas that were currently getting a second coat of pink paint. "All my friends are here, so I'm staying. All this shindig needs is some pizza and beer."

Linc ambled over. "I'll do the grub run."

"Call Ginos, and he'll have someone run it out here," Allen replied as he swiped some paint off his arm.

"Done," Linc said as he slid his phone out and walked away.

Zane picked up several of his tools. "Appreciate you getting the men to help out."

"That's what we do here," Allen answered as he looked up at the ride. "And let's be honest, this monstrosity is likely going to end up in one of the town parks, so it's an investment in Haven as much as you and Olivia."

"Me and Olivia?" he asked. "This ride doesn't have anything to do with us."

"Of course, it does." Allen rocked back on his heels. "It was the excuse you two needed to be in each other's company. It was a convenient cover that allowed you to explore the attraction while pretending otherwise."

Zane scoffed. "Olivia doesn't need a cover. The woman doesn't possess a single subtle bone and broadcasts her thoughts at full volume."

"I was talking about you, Zane."

"Oh," he said quietly, not sure where to take the conversation next. "I hadn't given any thought to where the ride would permanently reside. Guess I assumed it would stay here."

"Have you given any consideration to where you're going to permanently reside after the renovation is done on the house?"

"Initially, I planned to stay on and live a quiet life, filling my time with my antique clock restoration business."

"Sounds like you might've made some revisions to that plan."

Zane didn't want to be discussing his and Liv's relationship. That is if they still had one.

He'd been mucking it up fairly regularly with his growling and snarling and wouldn't be surprised if she wanted no part of him. "Still planning on staying. It's just the quiet part that won't likely happen."

"A full life is rarely a peaceful one." Allen crossed his arms. "You know, this is never an easy day for Olivia, so don't worry too much if she was out of sorts earlier. She's as strong as any woman I know and never lets herself simmer in the grief for too long."

Not wanting to admit his earlier transgression, he kept his mouth shut. How could he have picked a fight on one of her most challenging days? And why didn't she tell him beforehand how significant the day was?

It seemed he wasn't the only one with their drawbridge partially drawn.

"Food and libations are on the way," Linc called out.

"Thanks, cousin."

"No problem." Linc hooked his thumb over his shoulder. "I'm gonna get one more gondola painted before the chow arrives."

"Yeah, I'll do the same," Allen added.

Zane watched both men stride away and acknowledged once again that his demons needed to be evicted once and for all. There had to be a way to get rid of the lousy bunch of them along with his annoying dead relatives, didn't there?

He studied his hands and thought about the things he'd done in the name of freedom. The lives he'd ended of the country's enemies and the men who'd done their level best to do the same to him. Blah, blah, blah, he was tired of the reel of his sins that played continuously and was about ready to quit paying the Devil his due.

Letting out a gust of air, he crouched down in front of the engine box and vowed to double down on his efforts to get his mind right.

Olivia deserved better than what he'd been offering, and, one way or another, he needed to find a way to upgrade his emotional literacy.

Several hours later, the sun had dipped low enough in the sky to make any further work on the project impossible, so Zane collected the last of the detritus from their pizza feast and shoved it into a bag. His phone chirped in his pocket, and he was surprised to see Lucy's name on the display. "Hey, everything okay?"

"Not really," she replied. "Can you run over to Greenville and bring Olivia home?"

"Of course, is she okay?"

"As good as she can be on this day. She doesn't feel up to driving, and I can't go out there. I've got a water leak at the bookstore and am waiting on the plumber. I'm afraid if I leave, a pipe will pop, and my books will have to learn how to swim."

"I'll send Linc over. He's a contractor and can fix just about anything."

"No!" Lucy shouted.

He pulled the phone away from his ear. "Okay…but he knows what he's doing."

"I'm sorry; I didn't mean to screech in your ear. It's just that I've put a call into Ron, and he promised he'd come as soon as his wife has their baby and…"

"Lucy, did something happen between you and Linc?"

"Of course not! Why would you say that? Did he say something? Because if he did, it's not true, and…I didn't kiss him back. I merely stumbled, and that's why my lips landed on his." She let out a groan. "And to suggest otherwise is a bald-faced lie. Where else could I put my hands, anyway? It's not like I have the balance of a flamingo. A person does have to anchor themselves, after all. And…"

"Lucy, I get it."

"There is nothing to get. And he started it."

"Absolutely."

"Do you want to know where Olivia is, or do you want to continue to interrogate me about one mishap that lasted less than a minute and is barely memorable?"

"I'm ready for the intel."

"Good, because she doesn't need to be stranded at the Pink Pig."

"Text me the address, and I'll jump in my truck now."

"Okay. And thank you, Zane."

"In the meantime, I'll tell Linc to stop by because last I heard, books and water don't mix so good." A long sigh filled his ear.

"Fine. But only because my life's work is at risk. Not because I want to see that confounding man's face."

"Didn't think otherwise." He heard the call end and shook his head, knowing that his cousin had met his match in Lucy Bennett. It seemed he wasn't the only one who about to get schooled in the intricacies of taming a tiger.

\*\*\*

Olivia watched her porch lights come into view and was instantly comforted. "Thanks for the ride, Zane. I just couldn't stomach spending the night at the Motor Inn. The orange bedspread would have been one too many atrocities for my delicate constitution."

"You sure it doesn't have anything to do with the amount of tequila you consumed instead?"

She gingerly turned her head. "Can one ever be completely sure?"

"I guess not." He slid his hand across the console, linking their fingers. "And there's no thanks necessary. I would cross the goddamn Earth if you needed a ride or a rescue."

"That's so, so lovely." A faint smile crossed her lips. "Complete bullshit. But truly sweet."

"Just because I'm no good at this whole boy, girl thing doesn't mean that I wouldn't ride to your rescue without a second thought."

"I have no doubt." She squeezed his hand as he parked the truck. "Saving a damsel in distress is a side hustle you would certainly excel at. It's the other stuff that trips you up." The silence that followed her statement let her know that spouting her truth willy-nilly probably wasn't a good idea.

The mighty mezcal had loosened her lips and made what small filter she had disappear. She gave him a tight smile. "Thank you again. I'll make you some cookies or something."

"Don't treat me like a damn stranger, Liv."

Sitting up, she felt her head swim. "I don't bake for strangers."

"You know what I mean."

"No, Zane, I don't." She made a split-second decision and clamored over the console. Banging her head twice, she hoped not to end the evening with a concussion. "I need you to spell it out. Very slowly." She pressed her finger into his drawn brows. "Consider it a parting gift."

"I don't want to part, you infuriating woman. Quit trying to get rid of me."

"Me?" she sputtered. "It's you who is constantly backpedaling." She leaned in, feeling her Bennet temper rising like lava. "How dare you put this on me!"

An air of expectation filled the cab of the truck, and she didn't know where the tide of their emotions was going to take them.

Would they screw each other's brains out or shout down the trees?

Zane's bristling energy pushed against her chest, and she decided that more words were not going to solve their differences.

"You want to fix this by having some raunchy car sex, don't you?" Zane asked quietly.

"Don't pretend like it's a bad idea." She pushed her hands under his T-shirt. "We've been swinging from *all loved up* to *can't pick a fight quick enough*. For all we know, sex could fix it." She ran her mouth over his corded neck and felt her big bad warrior shudder. The way he gave in when she least expected it was no small thing.

Showing his vulnerability and giving her a glimpse of his need, no matter how unintentional, was a brave act. Something she wasn't confident that she had managed herself.

She let the notion take one lap and then decided it was more than her tired brain could manage at the late hour. It might be best to use the last of her energy to seduce the man and have one last glorious tumble.

She mentally tried to choreograph exactly how she could have her way with him in the truck and couldn't quite work out the details.

"Liv…"

Dragging her mouth away from his warm skin, she looked up. "Yes?"

"Let's go in the house."

"Let's stay here."

"No way."

She pushed her hair out of her face and sat up. "Well, that's disappointing."

"Having sex in the car doesn't make it mean less." He tilted his chin toward the house. "Let me take you inside."

"Why are you raining on my sexcapades?"

"You've had a lot to drink." He cupped her cheek. "And it's a damn difficult day for you."

"Are you denying me some sexual healing?"

"Nope." He opened the truck door and climbed out while managing to hold on to her. "But we're not going to do it in the truck. I want to see your eyes and make sure it's me you see and not some ghost."

Pushing herself out of his arms, she landed on her feet and swayed slightly. "I don't care for what you're implying, Zane. I'm not trying to use you as a substitute."

"If that's true, then you shouldn't be opposed to going upstairs."

She gave him a once over. "I don't know if I want you to come in, after all."

"No take-backs." He lifted her into his arms and strode in the direction of the front door. "If you want it, we're doing it in the bedroom."

The weight of the day crashed on her heavy heart, and she leaned her head against his chest. "I don't know why you've suddenly decided to be so formal. It's not like you'll spend the night."

"Do you want me to stay?"

"I didn't think it was an option since you always disappear before the sun comes up." She gripped Zane's arm as he opened the door and carried her over the threshold. Bella gave her a frown and then pushed her head against the doggy bed. "I think my dog just passed judgment."

"Welcome to my world. Killer is forever giving me the side-eye when I evict him from my lap."

Olivia wiggled and felt Zane's grip tighten. "I can make it up the stairs. And really, I'll be fine on my own."

"Liv, I haven't slept over because I don't want you to deal with my nightmares."

"Do you have them every night?"

"Just about," he answered as he ascended the stairs.

"I'll take the risk if you will."

A kiss was pressed to her head, and she hoped it was a yes. If he wasn't going to let her escape into sexual oblivion, then she would take his warm body holding hers.

Even though he wasn't likely to be around for very much longer.

Did that make her the biggest ninny in all the land? Perhaps, but that wasn't a truth that needed to be examined at one in the morning.

## CHAPTER NINETEEN

Zane opened one eye and squinted into the sunlight pouring through the window. Opening the other, he realized where he was and couldn't believe he had slept through the night.

An occurrence that only happened rarely.

Did it have anything to do with the snoring beauty in his arms? Pulling Olivia closer, he knew it most certainly did.

His mind was remarkably clear and quiet. It seemed he'd skipped his usual visit to the dark corners of his mind and allowed himself a night off.

What a relief.

Running his hand over Olivia's soft skin, he inhaled her scent, knowing that he'd never been as intimately entwined with another human. She had somehow managed to do what no other woman had and burrowed under his skin and into the beating muscle in his chest.

He spooned her closer, knowing it wouldn't disturb her rest, and snapped a mental picture of the red highlights in her wild morning hair. Tucking his knees into the back of hers, he let peace wash in and told himself there had to be a way for them to be good for each other.

What kind of hills did he need to climb to become capable of the kind of love the woman deserved?

He had very few clues and knew that's why he'd always avoided serious entanglements. Easy in and easy out had been his motto.

Until Olivia Elaine Bennett showed up on his doorstep.

Memories of Mosul unexpectedly began crowding in, so he closed his eyes, buried his face in Olivia's hair, and took long slow breaths. He pushed away the echoes of exploding bombs and replaced them with memories of Olivia's shouts of pleasure. The ones he'd given her when he'd driven himself into her addictive heat.

Relief slowly replaced terror, and he continued to replay each moment of their lovemaking. "Better," he whispered, remembering the way her touch soothed his ragged edges.

Hearing a murmur, he felt her press her ass against his lap. "Good morning to me," he muttered as his balls tightened. He thickened along the inside of her bare thigh and gripped the generous curve of her hip.

"You stayed," Olivia whispered.

"I did—hope it's okay."

"Silly man, of course, it is." She turned and pressed a kiss to his chest.

How was this his life? "Should I get up and make the coffee?"

"In a minute."

After biting her lip, she pushed him on his back, and he found himself mesmerized as her beautiful breasts swayed. He leaned up and managed a quick nibble before she snapped the sheet out of the way.

"My turn."

"Liv…"

"Hush."

Dropping his head against the pillow, he growled when her hand fisted his dick with confidence.

Instantly, his stomach filled with pressure as she gave him a tight stroke and then another.

Lifting his head, he tried not to pass out when he saw her mouth wrap around his girth. Olivia's beautiful lips brushed over the head, followed by her tongue. His balls felt like they might explode. "Damn…"

Another light lick had his hips jumping off the bed and his vision blurring. He fisted the sheets and told himself absolutely under no circumstance to drive himself into the sweet heat of her mouth. Moaning, she took at least four inches and tightened her lips, and she dragged them back up to the tip. "That's so good, Liv."

Humming, she moved back down his length, and he decided that anything less than full worship would not do when it came to his Olivia.

His nerve endings exploded like bombs beneath his skin. Every stroke went directly to his belly and sped him toward a climax. He dug his toes into the mattress as his hips thrust slow and nasty. Opening his eyes, he saw his girl's lips stretch as she sunk down to his root, her beautiful eyes on him the whole time.

Was she turned on too? The light in her eyes suggested she was. Through some miraculous effort, he held back his climax and roared, "Come here, Liv." He manhandled her, so she was sitting on his chest and facing away. "Go ahead; you can resume your torture now."

He got a sassy smile in response and then watched her bend forward, wrapping her mouth over his pulsing erection. Not wasting a minute, he tugged her hips back just enough. "So wet, babe. Is that what sucking me off does to you?" He greeted her with his tongue and stroked her tiny nub up and back slowly.

She gave him a low groan as she worked his length. Damn, he loved having her ass in the air as he licked her sweet honey. Good freaking morning to him. Her thighs trembled as she went for broke on his dick; whimpering, she sucked down to the base as he lashed his tongue against her bundle of nerves again and again.

His breath labored, he pumped his hips and doubled his efforts, swearing that he would taste her release before he gave in.

"Zane!"

She ground against his mouth, and cum shot out of his cock so fast he almost lost consciousness. Flicking his tongue with more intent, he gripped her hips and was rewarded with her release. He bucked and writhed as his body released its seed into Olivia's warm mouth.

Catching sight of the two of them in the mirror over the bureau, he watched Olivia's hand pump down his length as white drops of his cum landed on her chest. Another round of spasm seized him and turned him inside out. "Liv..."

Once he crashed back to earth, he sat up and wrapped her in a bear hug, promising once again somehow to become worthy of the incredible woman and grab as much happiness as he could.

\*\*\*

Olivia gingerly sat up and decided that she would live another day. Tequila, loss, and incredible goodbye sex were not going to be the end of her. She was made of sterner stuff and would be in full recovery mode before long.

"You're alive," Lucy announced from the doorway. "Though whatever is happening to your hair makes me think that might not be best."

"If I had more energy, I'd throw something at you."

"I'll make coffee. I brought a tray of cinnamon rolls; can you drag your fanny downstairs?"

"For sugar? Absolutely!"

Lucy scrunched her nose. "On second thought, take a shower before you come down."

"That bad?" Olivia asked as she pushed herself out of bed.

"Yes!"

She blew her sister a kiss. "I'll be down in a bit."

Ignoring Lucy's questioning glance, she walked into the bathroom and told herself there was no crying in baseball or at the end of a tryst with her neighbor. At least she assumed that's what their morning activities signified since Zane hadn't stuck around for a chat and left before she woke up from the orgasm-induced nap.

As far as she knew, they were in the same place and on the precipice of calling the game.

Was that dread or relief filling her heart? She couldn't tell.

Feeling at least fifty percent better, Olivia walked out of her bedroom and saw her sister's suitcases sitting outside the guest room. "Interesting."

She clomped down the stairs and entered the sun porch. "Are you running away from home?"

Lucy looked up from the book she was reading. "The water pipes are acting up, and Linc said shutting off the water was the only answer." She set down her book. "I'm not sure how long it's going to take to have everything repaired."

Olivia collapsed into a soft chair. "You know that you can stay as long as you like."

"Thanks, sister. Mom wasn't all that happy that I didn't choose to return home."

"Does her parrot still freak you out?"

"Yes!" Lucy filled their coffee cups. "I'm sorry, but that animal has no manners and says the most annoying things. Every time I'm over there, I feel those beady little eyes follow me around the kitchen as it squawks profanities."

"That bird sure can throw around a lot of judgment for such a small animal. It usually curses me out whenever I stay for more than an hour."

Lucy pushed the sugar in Olivia's direction. "I still don't know why Mom decided that rescuing the animal was necessary."

"Elaine Bennett has the biggest, softest heart, and there was no way she was going to let that bird be put down or sent to the glue factory."

"I know, and please don't rat me out if that bird eventually disappears under questionable circumstances."

"If you spill the delicious details of whatever is going on with you and Linc, then I promise to look the other way when feathers fly."

Lifting a cinnamon roll, Lucy frowned. "Nothing to tell."

"A lie if ever there was one." She pinched off a piece and slid it into her mouth, letting the sugar dissolve against her tongue. "But I can see you're not ready to discuss it, so I will wait patiently."

"Thank you," Lucy replied quietly. "I'm hoping that if I ignore the man, he'll simply disappear and take whatever black magic he possesses with him."

"After he fixes the pipes in the bookstore."

"Yes, after that." Lucy pushed her plate away. "And what is your plan for the recluse at the end of the lane?"

"I may take a page from your book and see what happens."

"And here I thought he had you properly sexed-up and contented as a kitten."

She let out a sigh. "He's minutes away from delivering some sort of, *it's not you, it's me* speech."

"The state of your bedroom and, if I'm not mistaken, your heart, notwithstanding."

"A mere pit-stop on the road to disaster."

"I don't like this new you." Lucy shook her head. "I much prefer your rainbows and happy puppy approach to life. All this doom and gloom doesn't suit you one bit. That's Callie's groove, not yours."

"Seems Zane is inspiring a new point of view."

"If Mom or Grams were here, they'd have something wise and prophetic to say—a metaphor about new love and old pain."

Olivia slid her finger through a glob of sugar. "They'd tell me that I'm not afraid of new love but old pain."

"And are you?" Lucy asked, "Afraid of giving Zane something you can't afford to risk a second time?"

"Probably. But I'm going to hunker down behind my emotional walls and invite denial over and see if I can hide from the truth for a bit longer." She folded her legs and leaned her head on her knees. "Why did I think that sexy times with Zane would be inconsequential?"

"You didn't," Lucy said quietly. "You merely decided that the reward of having even a small part of him outweighed the risk."

"Which is why staying away from sexy men is an idea we should embrace," she stated firmly.

"As much as something like that is possible."

Olivia lifted her head and studied her sister. "You have to give me a little tidbit. Linc is the opposite of every man you've ever dated, and I've never seen you so flustered." She leaned over and took her sister's hand. "Tell me the truth, how tempted are you?"

"A lot more than I'm comfortable admitting."

Knowing that sort of admission cost the always in control Lucy greatly, she nodded. "Then we won't discuss it further. Let's both hang out with our new friend, denial, and see how far it gets us."

"And if that doesn't work, we can always take a long road trip."

"Now, there's a good idea." Olivia let her feet fall to the ground and hoped that the Hawker men didn't have the means to blow up the Bennett sisters' careful defenses.

Something like that would be dangerous for everyone concerned.

## CHAPTER TWENTY

Race day dawned with a lot more gloom than Olivia expected. Sighing, she lifted a large tray of brownies and pushed through the screen door. At least the day's activities would make Zane show his face at some point. He'd continued to whipsaw from one extreme to the other, and she never knew which personality was going to be on display.

One thing she was certain of, though, was that she was about done with the nonsense. If he didn't give her the old heave-ho soon, she might just craft her own speech.

Her neighbor was mercurial at best and infuriating at worst and guessing which way the wind was about to blow had lost its appeal.

It was time to return to her staid and boring life. She was done with Zane squawking about the future one minute and being shut tighter than a pickle jar the next.

Love drama wasn't her thing and she didn't know how some people managed it on a semi-regular basis.

She shook off her angst and strode over to the snack table that Lucy was setting up. "Are you ready to start loading it up with treats?"

Lucy leaned over and smoothed out a wrinkle in the tablecloth and then nodded. "Drop those chocolate beauties here, and I will do my best not to eat them all before everyone shows up."

"On a scale of one to ten, how much chocolate therapy are we talking?"

"Twelve," Lucy replied as she took the tray out of her sister's hand. "And if I have to spend the day in Linc's company, then it will surely double."

"My goodness, I've never known a man to have that kind of power over the indomitable Lucy Aurora Bennett."

"Shut up," Lucy replied with little heat as she shifted the tray so that it was centered. "And for anyone interested, this is just an anomaly and will disappear as quickly as any spring storm."

"The Bennett sisters are batting a thousand," Olivia said quietly. "It might be time to take another look at the nunnery."

"They'd never let us in since there's no way to atone for the sins we commit on an almost daily basis."

"Speak for yourself," Olivia quipped. "Oh wait…the last time Zane and I were together, we knocked out at least three."

Lucy arranged her pile of necklaces carefully and then dropped her sunglasses. "We're not particularly lucky in love, but that doesn't mean we can't find a suitable hobby that would keep us away from trouble and heartbreak."

"I can't disagree, but reading, drawing, and drinking are all we're good at." Olivia looked up at the Ferris wheel. "Not that our interests can't be expanded."

"It's so much easier to be flippant because if you or I ever admitted how much we feel, we'd end up in a sea of emotions neither of us is capable of navigating."

"Agreed. The Bennett women have the unfortunate habit of loving too much. What other

TRUST

choice do we have but to numb ourselves to it just a bit?" Olivia stated firmly. "If we gave in, it would destroy us."

"Especially when they run off, never to be heard from again."

"Or die," Olivia said quietly.

Lucy wrapped her arm around her sister and squeezed tightly. "Or that."

"Okay, enough. We have lots to do, and unveiling the majestic beauty that inhabits my backyard is the least of it."

Lucy let out a whistle. "It looks like Betsy got herself a new look."

Olivia looked up and then clapped. "Well done, friend."

Betsy twirled around. "I took your advice, Liv, and am ready to move on."

"Good for you," Lucy said as she embraced Betsy in a hug. "Do you have a lucky candidate in mind?"

"I have several dates set up for next week and am thinking about taking a teaching position in Greenville next year." She swept her hands up. "I need to expand my horizons. I've had a crush on a man for five years and have wasted way too much mascara on someone who barely notices me."

"Amen," Olivia responded. "You are lit up from the inside out, and it's clear that letting go of an unrequited crush was the right answer."

Betsy smoothed her hand over her new bob and snorted her agreement, the sound exploding across the yard. "I'm not waiting for Hoyt a minute longer."

"Which means this is the exact moment he'll wake up." Lucy turned to her sister. "Do we have the paramedics on call?"

"I think so," Oliva answered.

"We better make sure, since the oldest Doherty brother is likely to have a heart attack the minute he gets a glimpse of the men who will be fawning over this one." Lucy squeezed Betsy's shoulder. "I love nothing more than seeing a man forced to feast on his errors."

"Very mature," Olivia retorted. "If Bea were here, we'd get a lecture on soul evolution, emotional intelligence, karma, and several other things that involve our chi."

Betsy pursed her lips. "Then we won't mention it when she arrives."

"Speak of the devil, here's our beloved sorceress," Olivia said as Bea parked her truck. "Hey, beauty!"

Bea waved and then pulled out a large tote. "I've brought everything we need."

Olivia, Lucy, and Betsy looked at each other.

"Don't worry, ladies; this day will not end in regret, embarrassment, or a trip to jail," Bea announced as she joined the group of women. "We may be about to face our greatest challenges, but I have sage, crystals, candles, and small pouches prepared specifically for each of you."

"Guess I shouldn't ask what's going on with you and Asher," Olivia said gently.

Bea emptied the bag on the table, picked up the sage, and ignited it with a lighter she produced from her pocket. Waving the burning herbs around, she smiled. "Nothing to report."

TRUST

"You may excel at the whole spiritual mastery thing, but you suck at lying," Lucy replied as she arranged the colored candles. "Are these repelling or attracting candles? Because I want to make sure to get a repelling one." She snatched the lighter out of Bea's hand, barely missing the sage she was waving around. "I don't need an inked up anti-prince with enough chill to be unnerving."

Betsy grabbed a pink candle. "I'll take an attracting one." She waved the sage smoke out of her face. "I want as many options as I can get."

Olivia picked up two and studied them. "I'll take one of each."

The sound of a truck filled the yard, and Betsy groaned. "I'll take a repelling one too because Hoyt just arrived, and I don't need him polluting my new vibe."

Lucy groaned. "Let's light these babies up; here they come."

Olivia turned and swore she heard a low drumbeat as all three Hawker men strode down the lane in a fog of testosterone. "This isn't going to end well."

Betsy lit the candles quickly and then handed the lighter to Bea, who lit the second bunch of sage. Olivia grabbed a pouch with her initial on it and shoved it into her pocket. "Just remember, we can call on the Haven Ladies' Society if we need to."

"And let them have all the fun?" Lucy snorted. "No way."

Saying a silent prayer, Olivia hoped that whatever happened gave her some closure. The angst of not knowing where Zane's affection lay on any given day was no longer something she wanted to tolerate. She blew out the pink candle and decided that for now, she was ready to repel the man that very nearly got ahold of her heart.

*\*\*\**

Zane accepted a cooler from Hoyt and stacked it with the others. "What do you say? Think we've got another half an hour before the runners finish their first lap?"

Hoyt jumped down from his truck and brushed off his hands. "Sounds about right."

Zane gave the quiet man a tilt of his chin and was surprised that he'd received a three-word answer. They'd been working on the water station set up for the last thirty minutes and hadn't exchanged ten words. The gentle giant had been far too preoccupied marking Betsy Yarlin's every move to engage in idle chit chat and he hoped to eventually discover the reason why.

Though, how that was going to be possible, he couldn't say since he and Liv had been taking turns avoiding each other. They'd barely spent fifteen minutes in one another's company in the last week and were advancing and retreating, with neither of them doing what the other expected.

The next move was probably his to make, and damn if he could force himself to do it.

For the first time in his life, he wanted nothing more than to avoid a confrontation. And that's exactly what he'd be stepping into since Liv's patience had probably run out. No doubt she had an impressive, *it's been fun speech* ready to go.

Hearing a sharp bark, he glanced up and saw Killer trotting in his direction. Bella sat next to the porch and gave him a confident look of triumph. Seemed both he *and* his dog were out of favor with the ladies of the house.

"Is that one yours?" Hoyt asked as Killer jumped over a small puddle.

"Yes. And I'm not sure I can get rid of him without a lot of blowback."

Hoyt bent over and scooped up the animal. "Not a fan of small dogs, but this one isn't bad."

Zane ignored the dog's look of disapproval. "Olivia decided I was the perfect dog-dad for the little beast and made me adopt him."

"Maybe, I shoulda gotten Betsy a dog or something." He stroked the dog's head. "Or just not acted like a complete idiot."

Zane crossed his arms over his chest and hoped that the story was about to be unraveled.

"You mind if I borrow..."

"Killer?" Zane finished.

"Yeah, I'm gonna show him to Betsy and see if she might want one."

Zane waved his hand. "Keep him as long as you like."

"Thanks, man, I gotta come up with something because she's been avoiding me." He hoisted the dog closer to his chest. "You'd think a woman that taught first grade would be a lot more understanding with someone who didn't handle unexpected declarations very well. A person that spends time teaching kids how to read should have a whole well of patience and not run off at the first opportunity and get themselves a new look, a half-dozen dates, and be talking about moving to the next town over." He sucked in a breath. "What has happened to teachers? Do they think every man has the social skills of those idiots who go on *The Bachelor*? Some of us haven't had a lot of practice, and it would be nice if women gave us a chance to get comfortable with the situation first."

Not sure if he understood the rambling confession or was expected to respond, he tried to appear sympathetic.

Hoyt slapped Zane on the back. "Thanks for the advice, Zane."

"No problem. He watched the man lumber in the direction of his heart's desire. "God bless you both."

"What's that?" Asher asked as he strolled up.

"Just dispensing pearls of wisdom wherever they're needed."

Asher let out a loud snort. "No, really, what's going on?"

"Great question, brother!" Zane adjusted his ball cap. "Feel free to enlighten me on your plans."

"I'm heading back to Virginia. I've got to finish the process of formally separating from the Navy."

"Are you going to return to Haven after you're done and hang up a shingle?"

"Yeah, I've got a lease signed on some office space." He looked around at the crowd. "There's only one other attorney in town, and he's about a hundred and twenty if he's a day. This town is ready for new blood and can use my skills."

"Glad you think so," Zane replied. "You ever gonna tell me what went on between you and Bea?"

"Nothing happened!"

He gave his brother a slow once over. "Yeah, I'm not buying it."

Asher slid his aviators out of his pocket and put them on. "Don't let that sage-waving yogi fool you. She might appear to be peace-loving, but she's really a steam roller that gets her way no matter what." He let out a frustrated growl. "Never underestimate the power of Namaste, brother."

"Wasn't planning on it." He tugged his phone out of his pocket and held it up. "Let me just get a quick picture."

Asher smirked. "What the hell for?"

"Posterity. This is the first time in recorded history that a woman hasn't fallen all over herself to get your attention." Zane pressed the button and hoped he captured Asher's disgruntled expression. "In fact, it looks like she's avoiding you at all costs."

"Whatever, I'm out."

Zane watched his brother storm away. "See ya, Romeo."

He took a quick look around to see if anyone else needed his wise counsel and spotted Olivia. Perhaps it was time to make an opening shot and put himself in the eye of the storm. Striding in the direction of the Ferris wheel, he hoped they could somehow find a way to give each other some peace—a safe space to rest their battered hearts.

Before he reached his destination, the two kids from the fair skidded to a stop in front of him, with Zelda following close behind. "What's up?"

"Ms. Olivia said you were in charge of the Ferris wheel," Sammy announced loudly.

"We want to be the first to go on," Kelsey added.

Sammy dug into his pocket and pulled out two quarters. "I got money and everything."

"Is that all you have?" Kelsey sniffed as she delicately extracted a fresh dollar bill from the panda purse that swung on her arm. "I've got more and will probably go twice."

"Liv is in charge of the high finance, so you two need to talk terms with her."

"They're not letting you out of their sights," Zelda said flatly. "You might as well let them go on. Otherwise, they're going to shadow you for the rest of the day."

"Are you in charge of these two hellions?" Zane asked with a laugh.

"For the next," she checked her watch, "hour and forty minutes."

"Hope you're getting top dollar for your efforts."

Zelda rolled her eyes as only a teenage girl could. "Would I be doing it if I wasn't?"

"She's saving for a car, so she and her friends can escape this tiny town and all the boring boys who hang out at the skate park," Kelsey added helpfully.

Zelda groaned. "You are not supposed to be listening when my friends and I are talking."

"You guys sound like screecher monkeys, so it's kinda hard not to," Sam said flatly.

"What have we got here?" Linc asked as he ambled up. "The great brain trust?"

"Are you the cousin that all the moms are talking about at the playground?" Sammy asked as he stepped closer to Linc. "A bunch of them were talking about you being bad in a good way." He swiped his hand over his nose. "What does that mean?"

Kelsey tugged on Linc's hand. "Zelda likes details, so use a lot of words." She leaned up on her toes. "Happy babysitter, happy life."

"I feel ya, girl. But have no idea what you're talking about."

Zelda snorted loudly. "I doubt that."

"Wow, Allen never mentioned that his delightful daughter had a side hustle in the intel game," Linc replied with a laugh.

Zane noticed Sammy copying Linc's stance. "Looks like you got an admirer, cousin."

Linc looked down. "Whatcha doing there, little man?"

"Copying you. I want to be bad but good."

"Might need a few more years before that's possible."

Sammy tipped his chin in the direction of Lucy and a group of women. "Which one you got an eye on?"

Linc ruffled the kid's hair. "A man never gives away his target. Best to keep that kind of information to yourself."

Kelsey glanced over at Zelda. "Who does he like? You know just about everything that happens in Haven."

Zelda gave Linc an arched eyebrow. "You want to tell them, or should I?"

"Jeez, girl, I've seen boat guys who don't have half your juice. And considering we like to fast-rope into a RIB that's hovering three-hundred and fifty feet above the ocean while the helo tries not to get weather vaned into kingdom come, that's saying something."

Zelda flipped a pink braid over her shoulder. "My mom says it's a gift and one I should use for good and not evil."

"Amen," Zane said quietly.

"I think he likes Ms. Lucy," Sam announced loudly. "You're gonna need a lot of funnel cakes to get her interested."

"Thanks, little Romeo, for the advice." Linc gave the small group a confident smile. "I got this."

"You so don't," Zelda snorted. "I heard the ladies chatting earlier, and repelling candle and your name were used in the same sentence."

"Not a big deal. It's an opposite attracts thing, and before too long, we'll have things worked out."

Zelda took Sam and Kelsey's hands. "I think it's more of an enemy to lover disaster in the making, but that's just me." She turned the children toward the ride. "We'll go stand in line for the Ferris wheel."

"Expect to be proven wrong, young lady," Linc called out loudly to the departing group.

"Got to be one of your proudest moments." Zane punched Linc in the arm. "I'm gonna leave now, so you can get your swagger back in place."

"Appreciate it," he mumbled before stalking in Lucy's direction.

Zane looked around for Olivia and didn't spot her. "Might as well handle the ride." He ran his hand over his neck and laughed, knowing that the Hawker men were skunking the game. No two ways about it.

## CHAPTER TWENTY-ONE

Oliva watched the sky light up with orange and yellow and let out her first full breath of the day. "Whew, that was a long one."

"Hey, babe, you ready for your inaugural ride?" Zane called out as he approached.

"If only that were possible," she replied regretfully. "I've got a thing with heights."

Zane rested his hand on her shoulder. "Why in the hell did you have me fix it then?" He bent over and peered into her face. "It was your dream, a shot at happiness."

"I know. But that doesn't mean I want to actually get in a gondola and be lifted fifty feet in the air and dangle precariously while I wait for the laws of nature to take over."

"If I'd known, I could've programmed it so it only lifts a couple of feet off the ground."

Olivia covered his hand. "That's lovely. But seeing everyone enjoy it today was all I wanted. Making something that was abandoned valuable again was my motivation."

"Feel like there's a metaphor in there that's meant for me."

"Not really." She stepped away. "I was broken for a long time and appreciate the people who never gave up on me—who saw that I was capable of more and one day would be whole again."

"Direct hit."

"Not intended as one." She let out a breath. "So, are you avoiding me, or am I avoiding you?"

"I think we're both spooked and acting accordingly," he said, taking her hand and leading her over to a bench that faced west.

"I've been waiting for you to say goodbye." She shivered and sat forward. "I know that I shanghaied you into an affair and will eventually craft a beautifully poignant apology for leading you astray."

"Liv, we both know that I can't be led anywhere. Least of all a place, I don't want to go."

"I was sort of hoping that you'd accept my theory that way I could heap some of the blame on your shoulders." She slid a ring on her finger round and round. "I want your lack of interest in an entanglement to be the sole reason why our little tryst is circling the drain slowly and somewhat painfully."

"Happy to take all the blame." He covered her hand. "But, I don't think our missteps have anything to do with my initial reluctance."

Olivia studied the harsh planes of Zane's face and admitted that he was always going to be a puzzle she couldn't put together. "I suppose it doesn't matter either way since we've taken a turn on the dance floor and found ourselves incompatible."

"We're a lot of things, but mismatched isn't one of them."

"If that were true, then you wouldn't be cantankerous one minute and staying away the next."

"I think you're reading the map wrong, Liv." He shook his head. "The truth is…the closer we get, the more I have to lose. I have never been this vulnerable in my life. And less capable of handling the unknown." He tightened his grip. "My uncertainty and fear are triggering a lot of bad behavior." Letting out a low grunt, he shook his head. "I'm sorry, Liv. You deserve a hell of a lot better than me."

"Thank you for the apology." She rested her head against his shoulder, feeling utterly defeated. If he didn't feel worthy, there was nothing she could do. "I admire how calm you are." She straightened and shifted away. "I'm a mess inside, and you're in total control. Must have something to do with your combat experience."

"Babe, going into battle is a lot easier than opening myself to what I'm fairly sure is utter destruction," his fingers gripped the bench, "of what's left of me."

"So, is it time to walk away from our short entanglement before we do too much damage to each other?"

"I don't want to, even though it's tactically the best option." Zane gusted out a big breath. "I gotta protect you, Liv. You deserve the best a man has to offer."

"Don't you dare drop your fear of failure in my lap." She moved to the edge of the bench. "Just admit that being single is your jam. Telling me that I need protection is a smokescreen that I won't let you hide behind." She squinted her eyes, making the colors in the sky melt together. "You got to me, Zane, in a way no one ever has."

"Same, Liv."

"Another life-changing declaration said with so little emotion." She let out a mirthless laugh. "It's like you're telling me about a plumbing issue or the expected weather for next week."

Zane dropped his head. "If I don't keep an iron fist on my emotions, then I'll blow something up or start howling at the moon."

Folding her hands carefully, Olivia swallowed all the feelings that being in Zane's company produced. There was no happy ending to their tale, and it was time to accept it. Trying to love a man who was tied in more knots than a macramé plant holder, was madness. And that wasn't anything she needed to take on.

She wasn't a fool for love, after all.

Especially with a man who had zero interest in exploring his vulnerability. Not that she was particularly enthusiastic about the prospect. But that certainly wasn't the point. Sighing, she closed her eyes and told all her soft emotions to take cover.

"I knew early on that the care and feeding of a woman like you was beyond me."

"What the hell does that mean?"

Zane lifted his head slowly. "You're not a good-time girl. You are the real deal and deserve a man who can commit."

"And who says that you don't have that to give?" She pushed herself to her feet. "Maybe the lie that you're not capable is one you invest in so that you don't have to risk losing again."

"That's rich, Liv. Especially coming from you."

"What the hell does that mean?"

"You ready for that kind of truth to be laid down?"

She leaned down, so their faces were close. "I have dealt with the hard cold truth for so long that I can't remember a time when I didn't."

He groaned. "I can tell by the look on your face that you don't truly believe that."

Fury filled her body, and she let it unfurl, knowing that any emotion was better than the pain radiating from her heart. She embraced the rush of adrenaline and was ready for a good brawl. Shouting and raising her fist to the injustice was much more appealing than examining the untruths she comforted herself with.

She fisted her hands and firmed her resolve, knowing she could handle anything the man had to share. "I'm listening, Zane."

***

Was he poking the bear? Absolutely.

Did he regret it?

Not even a little.

Olivia was hiding behind some well-constructed lies, and he was damn tired of it. "I'm not the only one with demons, Liv. You've got a whole bunch of your own. Thad's ghost is alive and well, and you're keeping him nice and close, so you never have to risk your heart again."

"How dare you!" she replied with a low, tight tone.

He stood, towering over her. "Oh, yeah…that's right, your emotional acuity can't be questioned. Happy, positive Liv doesn't have any hidden monsters that gnaw on her bones and make her question if truly opening herself up to another is a good idea." He slapped his heart. "It's just the scarred vet that has shit to work out."

Stepping forward, she pressed her finger into his chest. "You take that back."

He covered her hand and felt his anger drain away. "I can't, babe. You're just as frightened as I am. Your packaging is just a whole lot better and makes everyone, including yourself, believe that you're ready to move forward." Letting out a shaky breath, he moved closer. "I didn't pay close enough attention when you admitted that I could break your heart. I'm your litmus test, the same way you're mine."

"I don't want to take the damn test, Zane."

"I know, but it's been given, and our next move is going to determine whether we get a pass or fail."

Nothing, his little chatterbox was blinking furiously. If he had to guess, he'd say that she was trying to come up with a rebuttal that would light his ass on fire.

He crossed his arms and tried to make sense of the feelings rioting through his body. If he were more evolved, he'd be able to admit that it was anxiety and vulnerability. Two things he abhorred.

One way or another, he'd always found a way to dominate and flourish.

Until that op.

That wasn't an experience he needed to repeat. And being in an actual relationship with Olivia all but guaranteed it. How could he willingly walk into what was sure to be the second greatest failure of his life?

"Love isn't a test, Zane. It's a chance to be the best version of ourselves."

"Same thing."

She stepped in front of him and tugged on his arm. "Your past doesn't define your future. And I don't mean that in some bullshit greeting card way. Can't we always do better?"

"Yes. And I know that I should *just get over it*—bury the memories of the men I couldn't bring home alongside their corpses." He took her hand and squeezed. "I'm a fucking cliché. And there isn't a damn thing I can do about it."

"You're no such thing, Zane Hawker. You're merely mortal and paying the unimaginable price for the things your country asked you to do in the name of democracy."

"Don't give it a high shine, Liv. What I did with the men I served with was down and dirty warfare. We did the things so few could, and…"

"Made sacrifices," Olivia finished quietly. "But none of that is truly the reason you're walking away. So, let's not pretend."

"And what's making you walk away, Liv?" He tipped her chin, so they were looking at one another in the fading light.

"I'm smart enough to know that unrequited love is bullshit." She moved out of reach. "I can't continue to chase you, hoping that I'll someday be more interesting than the pain you keep close."

"Believe it or not, I've tried." He looked up at the sky and couldn't ignore the fact that her happiness was more important than his own. He had a lot of work ahead of him, and when he'd be on the other side of it, he couldn't say. How could ask a woman like Liv to wait?

"No," she whispered. "You allowed fear to be more important than love. Our fragile moments of connection triggered you, and instead of doing something about it, you're choosing to hunker down behind your walls. Well, enjoy troll life, Zane. And don't worry, I'll leave you be." She took a step back and then another. "I knew you were a lot of things, but I never thought being a coward was one of them."

He watched her stride toward the house and accepted that perhaps that's exactly what he was. Because if he weren't, he wouldn't let her walk away, taking his heart with her.

## CHAPTER TWENTY-TWO

Twelve days had passed since Olivia walked away from Zane, and she'd spent ten of them roaming the beach. The current day being the most relaxing. Soft sand cushioned her feet, the wind blew gently against her face, and the sun warmed her shoulders, making her question why she hadn't made the friendly beachside community home.

She'd hightailed it out of Haven hours after the confrontation with her lover and driven directly to her sister's house on the Outer Banks. Thankfully, Callie was elated to see her and welcomed her to stay for as long as she liked. An offer she had taken seriously.

They'd been cooking up a storm during the evenings and indulging in every feel-good movie that Netflix featured. It had been too long since she'd had uninterrupted time with her baby sister, and she was more grateful than ever that they both pursued their careers from home, albeit in diametrically opposed disciplines.

Callie was a genius programmer and did all kinds of work for government agencies that she couldn't and wouldn't name. Her faded yellow house that sat steps from the ocean was not the idyllic getaway that most people would suspect but headquarters for some high-level dark web something or other.

Bella gave her a happy bark, and she realized that she hadn't thrown the tennis ball yet. Pitching it as far as she could, she watched her girl thunder in the direction of the bright yellow ball and watched her snatch it out of the water right before a wave crashed against the shore. As she ran back with her prize, Olivia thought about Killer and hoped that Zane didn't offload the dog before she could find it a new home.

She'd made Lucy promise to keep an eye out for the little darling and take in the dog if her neighbor thought the pound was a viable option.

Not that she thought he would stoop so low. He wasn't heartless, after all. "Twenty-six," she said quietly as Bella dropped the ball and sat on her feet. She'd been keeping track of the number of times Zane came to mind, and the fact that she hadn't hit triple digits before lunchtime was an encouraging sign. "Road to recovery, Bella. We're definitely on it."

She collapsed onto the sand, adjusted her hat, and then leaned back. "Maybe we should stay here and become beach bums."

"You say that every time you visit," Callie remarked as she plopped down and handed Liv a bottle of water. "But we both know you'd miss Haven too much."

"I'm evolving, sis. It might be time to stretch my wings and strike out on a new adventure."

Callie swept her hair over her shoulder. "I wish that were true, but we both know you simply don't want to go home and see Zane on a semi-regular basis."

"I'm guessing my absence has allowed him to embrace his reclusive nature. He's probably gone full troll under the bridge and is having everything delivered to his door, so he never has to speak with another human again."

Callie chuckled. "I doubt that since you spent at least a day and a half describing in great detail all the friends he's made and his growing popularity."

"Thanks for pointing out that my hermit theory is full of holes." She stroked Bella's head. "I guess that means moving is the only answer."

"Or you could just go home and do the unimaginable."

She dropped her sunglasses. "And what might that be?"

"Face your fears. From everything you've told me, it sounds like you and Zane are doing the same dance of avoidance. For wildly different reasons, of course."

"I am not avoiding anything. I did everything short of prostrating my naked body on his porch to get him interested." She ran a hand through the sand and barely stopped herself from drawing a broken heart. "I was the pursuer and gave him little chance to avoid my romantic gestures."

"I'm sure a Green Beret could've found a way to avoid your naked bits and overtures if he wanted to. The few I've met could topple an insurgency without breaking a sweat."

"Wait, when have you met special operators?"

Callie turned her face toward the water. "That's not the point of this conversation, is it?"

She studied her beautiful blonde sister, who resembled a woodland sprite, and narrowed her eyes. "Are you going to tell me about your secret life anytime soon?"

Callie lifted her mouth into an innocent smile. "I'm just a programmer."

"That takes six-week trips abroad to undisclosed locations at the spur of the moment."

She grinned. "What can I say? Travel is my happy place."

"There's a Hawker brother that's in Black Ops; I wonder if you two run in the same circles."

Feigning a look of puzzlement, Callie took her sister's hand. "What did we decide to make for dinner? Should I run into town and pick up some crabs?"

"Fine," she said with a huff. "I'll change the subject."

"Let's get back to this neighbor thing and how you're going to take the universe up on its offer and face the thing you fear most."

"Are we talking about my dread that white cheddar Cheetos will sell out and I will be forced to start eating the puffs?"

"Nope. Not that one."

"Oh, then you must be referring to my terror of discovering a worldwide shortage of chocolate, then."

Callie raised an eyebrow. "I thought you could deal with the one that tells you that if you love someone thoroughly and without reservation, they will be taken from you."

"I'd rather leave that one in a locked box. It doesn't care for the light of day or really any careful consideration."

"And yet, happiness is all but guaranteed if you do."

"No, it's not, sister." She folded her hands. "I tried to love the lonely out of him, and it didn't work. What a fool I was."

"Now, we're getting somewhere." She covered Olivia's hands.

"He never really wanted to take me on. He said it in a dozen different ways, and I ignored every one, thinking that if I just gave a tiny bit more affection, he'd see that I was worth the risk."

"Did he give in just enough to make you believe it was possible?"

"Yes," she whispered against the wind. "He'd say the loveliest things out of nowhere, and as much as I told myself it wasn't possible…"

"A part of you believed it was because who in their right mind can ignore such tempting proclamations?"

"I started to love him, Cal." Turning toward her sister, she felt a tear slip down her face. "As best as anyone can when the person isn't yours."

"And Zane…what did he feel?"

"Lust," she replied firmly. "Because if it were anything more, he never would've let me go."

"I'm gonna channel Grams for a second, so don't get mad."

Olivia let out a strangled laugh. "Hit me, sista, with your best shot. I am as ready as I'll ever be."

"There's a difference between someone who is not actually choosing you and someone who is struggling to trust themselves enough to open their heart and be vulnerable. Maybe Zane is the latter and couldn't get out of his own way."

Feeling something that felt suspiciously like an arrow piercing her heart, she sucked in a breath. "That's something I never considered."

LEA HART

"Well, now's as good a time as any to do just that." Callie pushed herself to her feet. "I've got a couple more hours of work, so I'm gonna head in."

"Thanks for the wise words, Callie."

"Just remember Mom's favorite mantra; you can't screw up anything that is meant for you. If this thing with Zane is meant to be, then you'll find a way to work it out."

Olivia nodded and then watched her sister trudge along the sand toward her house. All the over-the-top gestures she'd made Zane endure allowed her to believe that she was ready to open herself up to the idea of love. But that wasn't the case at all.

She let fear corrupt her burgeoning feelings. The moment he announced he didn't want any part of her chaos, she folded her emotional tent and kept her soft heart under lock and key as best she could.

But she hadn't completely succeeded, had she?

Her grumpy neighbor owned a tiny corner of her heart, and she had no idea how to get it back. Maybe she could simply demand he return it. Tell him in no uncertain terms she wanted no part of his…anything.

It's not like he was some great prize with his stupidly handsome face, indomitable grit, and heart that, if ever left to its own devices, could love down the world. There were much better options out there, and she should start exploring them the minute she snatched her heart back from Zane.

He probably didn't even know he had it, so wresting it out of his grip shouldn't take much effort. "What do you say, Bella, should we go home and put our emotional house back in order?"

When she got nothing but a loud doggy snore, she lay back on the sand and put her hat over her face, thinking about what the next part of her life was going to look like.

When Zane's handsome face kept popping up, she let out a groan. "Nope, not going to take it as a sign. It's simply old programming, and all I have to do is make sure I come up with a fabulous new one." With great concentration, she mentally replaced Zane's face with Liam Hemsworth's. He could be her new boyfriend. All she had to do was run over to Australia and find him.

How hard could it be?

## CHAPTER TWENTY-THREE

It had been two weeks, and the loss of Olivia made the air around him feel stale and thick with loss. Zane pushed himself up, ran his hand over his scarred cheek, and looked around his bedroom. He let out a feral howl as the memory of one of her juicy suffocating hugs filled his mind. The window rattled in its casing, and he flipped off the family ghosts in response. "Too damn bad. If you don't like it, move on."

Linc pushed the door open. "You ready to move on to phase two?"

"Didn't know there'd been a phase one."

"The trash cans rattling with glass bottles should've given you a clue." He hitched his shoulder. "But then again, Army guys aren't all that bright, so it's not surprising."

Zane bounded out of bed and was ready to pummel his cousin. What a relief to feel something other than overwhelming regret and loss. The rage that filled his belly was welcome, and he guessed, if stoked properly, could last the day.

He cocked his arm back and was about to throw a right hook when he noticed that Linc looked bored. "Put your damn hands up."

"Nope. Not gonna do it." He scratched his chin. "I can't be fighting because I'm almost one hundred percent sure that I've got Lucy talked into a date. Got to keep this pretty face of mine bruise-free."

"A what?"

"Date. You know that thing men and women do when they like each other."

"But she barely tolerates you."

Linc chuckled loudly. "Which is an improvement from where I was last week. Things are looking up, cousin."

Adrenaline drained out of his limbs and he watched Linc saunter toward the stairs. "Son of a bitch. Won't even go one round with me."

"Call Hoyt Doherty," Linc called out. "The situation isn't working out with Betsy, and he's about as frustrated as you. You two can beat the hell out of each other because that's sure to fix the trouble y'all created for yourselves."

"I didn't..." Not able to finish the sentence, he stalked across the hall into the bathroom. He couldn't use the one attached to his room anymore because it was filled with memories of Liv. Stupid claw foot tub. It taunted him every time he entered and acted like a neon sign reminding him of what he'd lost.

Maybe he should rip the thing out and install some kind of shower with sixteen showerheads. That would surely fix what ailed him and ensure that he would be able to take a full breath at some point in the future.

Zane walked into the kitchen, ignored his cousin, and strode over to the coffee pot to fill his cup. Killer was hot on his heel as usual and parked his doggy behind at his feet. It turns out the little white ball of fluff excelled at standing sentry.

"Lucy reminded me that she would take Killer whenever you're ready. She and Olivia don't want the dog to end up at the pound or anywhere else."

"What kind of ogre do they think I am?"

"That's a rhetorical question, right?"

Zane strode over to the table and dropped into a seat. "Have you seen me without this dog for more than ten minutes since you arrived?"

"This isn't the right time to bring up that misunderstanding with Betsy and Hoyt, right?"

He lifted the dog into his lap. "I never said that he could give the dog to Betsy. It was a desperate man making a desperate mistake."

"And we're going to stick to that story no matter what."

"What are you still doing here, anyway?" Zane gulped his coffee. "You're usually at the bookstore by now."

"Lucy is going in a little later today, so I'm hanging back until she's ready to go."

"And she can't drive herself into town?"

"A question like that tells me exactly why you've been crying into your Cheerios and not loved up with your girl."

"My therapist would say that's projection."

"The fact that you've got a damn therapist is thanks to me, so I don't care what kind of psycho-babble you throw my way."

Zane stroked Killer's head. "I do appreciate you hooking me up with the guy. I never woulda thought of doing the phone sessions if you hadn't suggested it."

"Glad you're sticking with it," Linc replied.

"Losing the one person who makes the world feel okay kinda motivates a person to buckle down and face the stuff that made it possible."

"All the same. Not everyone takes the opportunity to do the work."

Not able to unjumble the emotions churning, he knocked fists with Linc and then drank more of his coffee.

"You know you're lucky."

"How's that?" Zane asked.

"A terrific girl came along and gave you all the good reasons to leave the past where it belongs."

"Too bad I wasn't ready for it."

"I doubt many people are, even if they haven't been in war."

"Guess that's possible."

Linc folded his napkin. "You know it is since you've seen every single man in this family struggle with the transition from life in the military to one at home. We've all spent years at the tip of the spear and brought darkness home like some horrible souvenir we should've left behind. Our souls tell us we don't deserve happiness because we lost brothers on the battlefield. And then our guts shout that it wouldn't be right to make something of the life we've been spared if they can't. Which is all total BS, make no mistake about it."

Zane let out a breath and watched his little dog press his head into his hand. "I mistakenly thought if I stayed buried under the layers of pain and guilt that it would do my fallen brothers some good."

"Same, cousin. I tried to tell myself that rolling around in my misery would show them that their sacrifice was worth something."

"How do so many of us get it all wrong?" Zane asked.

"Because we're not taught differently. There's no post-war training we can attend that gives us the tools to navigate the new normal."

"Amen to that."

"And let's face it, this thing between men and women is a whole kinda battlespace of its own. If you catch real feelings for a chick, then strap up because you are about to face the greatest test of your life."

"I failed that challenge spectacularly and lost the battle."

"You just had a lousy first round. The trick is to stay in. Fight for Olivia while she still gives a fuck because one day, you'll be too late."

"I might already be."

"Nah, a woman who looks at you the way Liv did needs a lot more than two weeks to fall out of love."

"Here's to hoping she's got some previous undetected well of patience because I've got a lot of work ahead of me before I'm worthy."

"Women don't want perfect. At least that's what Lucy alluded to the other day. They just want to know there's light at the end of the tunnel."

Was that possible? He sure hoped so because there was nothing he wanted more than another chance with his neighbor.

Even if he wasn't ready.

Linc heaved himself to his feet. "I'm gonna head out. Catch ya later."

"Yeah, later." The moment his cousin cleared the doorway, his phone buzzed, and he glanced at the display. "What the hell?" He answered the call immediately. "Birch, you son of bitch. I hope this call doesn't mean I have to rescue you out of some hell hole."

"Brother, I would call the team boys if that were the case, not some pansy-ass Green Beret."

"Good to know," he snorted.

"You okay?"

"Yeah, you know, just out here shaking shit up," Birch answered with a laugh.

"When you coming home?"

"Soon, brother."

Knowing Birch wouldn't call without a real good reason, he waited, hoping that whatever it was wouldn't require him to stand at another grave.

"Got some intel, and I wanted to pass it on."

"Oh, yeah…"

"Seems your girl is on her way home. My source suggested that you get your act together and do something called a grand gesture. Not sure what that means, but I was assured that you would understand."

Flummoxed, Zane sat back. Birch lived deep in the black-ops community, and he was fairly confident that few people knew that he was A, alive or B, how to get in touch. Since Olivia was up North with her baby sister, he couldn't see how those worlds bisected. "Any chance you'll reveal your source?"

"Nah. But when I get home, I expect to meet this lucky lady and get a full download on why my contact is so invested in the outcome."

"Don't think Olivia considers herself lucky, but that's a tale for another day."

"Hence the grand gesture, I'm assuming."

"Whatever the hell that is."

"Get on it, Z. Nobody is better than making something out of nothing than you." Birch chuckled into the phone. "I still remember how you got the toaster to shoot the bread far enough so we wouldn't have to get up from the table."

"That was some of my finer work."

"Not even close."

Zane heard his brother mumble something. "Everything okay?"

"Yeah, I gotta go do a thing."

"Stay frosty, Birch."

"Always."

The call ended, and he studied his phone and tried to puzzle out how his brother had come to dispense advice from across the globe. At least he assumed that's where he was. For all he knew, he was in Miami Beach sipping mojitos.

Grand gesture. What the hell was that?

Did it involve explosives or a bunch of flowers? He had no idea.

One thing he knew for certain was that it needed to include chips, chocolate ice cream, and wine. Olivia liked him best when she had all three available, so he'd be a fool not to have plenty on hand.

He glanced down at Killer. "Feel free to jump in with any ideas. I'm totally open." The dog dropped his head and let out a sigh of resignation. "Not the kind of support I was looking for."

No matter, he wasn't going to be put off. He'd been one of the better tacticians in his unit and coming up with something grand was certainly in his wheelhouse.

It couldn't be any harder than squashing an insurrection, could it?

## CHAPTER TWENTY-FOUR

Olivia watched Lucy wave goodbye from Linc's truck and prayed her sister didn't underestimate the confident smile the man wore. The oldest of the Bennett sisters had met her match and how that wasn't going to play out was anyone's guess.

Actually, that wasn't true. Olivia knew without a doubt that Lucy's road to happiness was going to be rocky, at best. And treacherous at worst.

"Bitter, party of one," she mumbled as she studied her reflection in the hallway mirror. She adjusted her lilac ribbon and silently repeated several positive affirmations. It was time to flip the switch and do what was necessary to excavate her neighbor from her heart and mind.

Romantic angst wasn't going to become her new best friend. No way. She had a fabulous life to create and the sooner she let Zane know that her heart was her own and he had no claim on even the smallest corner of it, she would be free.

Perhaps she'd go over later and inform him of the facts as she understood them and assure him that she would keep to her end of the lane and expected him to do the same. Once they were both absolutely clear on the new parameters of their relationship, there was no reason why they couldn't be civil. They were adults and both relatively mature, so it should be a breeze.

She smoothed out her bangs and pushed her mouth into a smile. "Right as rain."

Hearing a short knock on her front door, she peered through the kitchen window. No one was expected, and she hadn't heard a car, so she couldn't imagine who it could be. Walking slowly over to the door, she looked through the side panel. "Oh." She took several steps back and tried to slow her breathing. "Not a big deal. Might as well get it over with. No time like the present and all of that."

"Liv, I know you're in there."

*Darn it!* She wasn't quite ready.

Another soft knock told her he wasn't going away and would likely camp out on the front stoop until he had his say. Though what he had to share, she couldn't imagine. What with his whole recluse, *I need no one* thing.

"Whatever. I can handle this!" She opened the door and told herself she felt nothing. Not an ounce of regret, attraction, or any other emotion that would allow her resolve to soften. "Hey, neighbor. What brings you by?"

"I found one of your ribbons and wanted to return it."

"You didn't have to do that, Zane. I have dozens." Uncertainty swam in his eyes, and she ignored it with every fiber in her being.

She gave him a tip of her chin, reminding herself that it wasn't her job to make it better. Understand. Or offer solace. It was her *duty* to keep her walls fortified, so she didn't embrace the fool in a hug and do everything she could to take just a bit of his loneliness away. He had a dozen friends now that could do the job beautifully, and if she weren't mistaken, a pile of crumpled numbers somewhere.

He'd be fine. And so would she.

They just had to get over this rough bit, first.

She took the proffered ribbon and noticed he didn't let go. In fact, he tugged on it and moved her closer. The delicious heat that always seemed present when they were together was especially strong, and she did everything she could to ignore it. "You can keep it if you want to."

"I had a whole speech prepared."

Her grip on the lilac ribbon slipped, and instead of making him release it, it drew him closer. "Well, go on then. I'm listening."

"It was something…wasn't it?

Her heart skipped a beat, and she found none of the words floating in her brain able to be set free.

"It was for me," Zane said quietly. "And if it wasn't for you, then that's gonna be a hell of a pill to swallow." He took a step in. "You want to tell me everything I did wrong—I'll listen. But please, babe, don't keep quiet."

"It was something." She swallowed loudly. "But now, it's not."

"If I'm your greatest regret, then so be it because that's something I can build on. But if what we had was just a way to pass the time, then…"

"You know that's not what I was doing." She pushed her sandal across the floor. "Have you already forgotten all those unwelcomed overtures, I made?"

"Liv, you never did anything that wasn't one hundred percent welcome. Uncomfortable, absolutely. But that was because having a woman like you interested in any part of me simply didn't compute."

"That's some fine revisionist history, Zane."

"It's no such thing."

Praying her emotional walls could withstand the man's presence, she cleared her throat. "Netflix is killing it right now. I have plenty to keep me busy. I won't..." she waved her hand around, "bother you anymore."

"You haven't been listening, Liv."

"There are hours and hours of excellent programming that I'm dying to get started on."

"Make no mistake, Liv, I will find a way to become more interesting than a travel show." He let out a frustrated huff. "If you want to watch that regency romance thing a fourth time, I will happily sit next to you, and..."

"Why?" she whispered, frustration filling her chest. Why did men make the most infuriating proclamations the moment women were ready to walk away? "I'm not interested in a push-pull thing with you." She let go of the ribbon and watched it flutter against his hand. "You only seem to want my company when it's no longer available."

"Babe, that is not true." He linked their pinkies. "I told you from the beginning that I wasn't in any kind of mental or emotional shape to take you on. I want to be worthy and..."

"Love doesn't require perfection." She shook her head. "I think the very idea of being without fault is ludicrous. We are all worthy of affection and our foibles are what makes us lovable."

The corner of Zane's mouth tipped up. "If you mean that, then I could very well end up being the man of your dreams."

Some of the tension in her muscles drained. "I planned on telling you..." Bella's happy bark interrupted her thought. "Did you get rid of Killer?"

"No!"

"Don't overreact, jeez." She unlinked their fingers and smoothed out her skirt. "Considering you all but gave him away at the race."

"I did not! And you know it since I explained the misunderstanding. Hoyt asked to show the dog to Betsy to see if she might want one. How he interpreted that to mean he could put my dog on offer so he could remedy five years of romantic screw-ups is not something I can be held responsible for."

"That doesn't answer my question." She pushed past him and walked out to the yard. "Oh."

Zane joined her and let out a laugh. "Well, there you go."

"This isn't a sign, Zane."

"Babe, it sure the hell is."

Olivia let out a sigh and knitted her hands together. Bella and Killer were lying together in the shade of the Ferris wheel, friendly as can be.

"Those are some contented dog siblings."

"Oh, be quiet. I'm sure it's an anomaly," Olivia answered, knowing it was no such thing. Bella was as stubborn as she was, and if she was allowing the little white ball of fluff on her turf, then it meant something. But not what Zane thought.

"Go on, Liv. I can't wait to see how you're going to thread that needle."

She turned and gave what she thought was an impressive look of disinterest. "I want to state clearly, for the record, that I'm over my crush and will expect any hold you have on my affections to be released immediately."

"Yeah, that's not gonna be possible."

"Why?" She stomped her foot. "You have plenty of options."

"I've got a hell of a date planned for us. How does tomorrow sound?"

"A date?" Oliva asked. She closed her eyes and tried to determine if she was dreaming. When she felt Zane's arm brush hers, she decided it was a rabbit hole she'd fallen down. What other explanation could there be for him ignoring her clear communication?

"It's the thing men and women do together when they like one another," Zane said with patience.

Olivia opened her eyes. "I'm well aware of that, Zane. It's just that..." she ran her hand over her slick neck. How dare he make her so out of sorts? She was supposed to be a cool cucumber and the boss of the discussion. Instead, they were hopping around from one topic to another like rabbits on crack, never finishing one thought before they started on another. It was one of the most confounding encounters, she'd ever had. "We're not involved."

"Yes, we are."

"Why are you making this so difficult?" She let out a groan. "You should be doing a happy jig and running home to call any one of the interested women in town."

"There is only one, I care about and I'm trying to ask her out on a damn date so I can make a grand gesture, so she'll forgive me, and we can start again."

"Oh..." Olivia took a step back. "Well..."

"Is that a yes to 7:00 tomorrow?"

"No." She pinched her mouth together. "I want you to release my heart and..."

"No can do." He kissed her cheek. "You love giving old broken-down things a second chance, don't make me the exception." Taking her hand, he pressed it against his chest. "Let's show this town and ourselves why it always works out in the end."

"That's not fair, Zane."

"That's the thing about love and war; it's got nothing to do with fair." He smiled confidently. "And don't think for a second that I won't use every down and dirty tactic I know to get you to allow me a second chance."

She watched the muscle in his jaw tic as his gaze fastened on her mouth. Unbidden memories floated to the surface and she did what she could to ignore the voice in her head that said he was the one and always would be.

Zane ran his finger over her cheek. "One date, Liv. Please. Before you make a final decision."

"Fine," she huffed out, untucking her hand from his. "I'll go on one silly date but know that I've carefully tucked away my soft bits." She wasn't going to roll over and simply accept his words at face value. She gave him her best beady-eyed stare. "I acquired some nice new armor while I was away, so know that your efforts will likely fail." Her head throbbed and she let out a sigh. "I didn't tape my heart back together just to have it broken again."

"Understood."

"And, don't expect this little date to result in some happy ever after where we magically forget past transgressions. We're not going to have some kind of love epiphany and look at each other with hearts in our eyes just because a few sweet confessions were exchanged." She leaned back. "You are planning on some kind of sugary declaration of your feelings, right?"

"I'm not giving you the details of the battle plan, woman." He gave her a sad shake of his head. "I'm a damn spec operator with more medals than I know what to do with." He pressed a kiss to her head. "A rough start doesn't mean we can't kick love's ass. I always succeed, Liv and this ain't gonna be any different."

Not wanting to give him undue encouragement, she shrugged carelessly. "There's a first time for everything, Zane." She gave him a saucy smirk and then spun around and stalked toward her house.

It was a shame that it was too darn early for a drink because she could sure use one.

Or three.

## CHAPTER TWENTY-FIVE

Zane strode down the road and replayed the chaotic discussion that led to Olivia agreeing to a date and tried to pinpoint the moment when he'd worn her down. Not a positive way to view the situation, but what the hell...he was a work in progress.

A fact he was trying to get comfortable with each and every day.

He ran his hand down the front of his dress shirt and told himself he was more than ready to show Olivia that he was worth the gamble. No more wishy-washy bullshit. He was going all in. Damn the consequences.

He glanced down at Killer. "Be on your best behavior, little man. Don't annoy Bella and nip at her heels. We're showing those Bennett women that the men from the Hawker family are the gold standard." The little white dog barked out an agreement and trotted along like he was in the Westminster dog show. "Easy now. We're the supporting players, not the stars."

Olivia's house came into view and he gripped the bouquet. "Show time." His phone pinged with an alert and he checked it quickly. "Looks like supper was delivered. The stage is set."

He strode up to Olivia's door and pressed the doorbell, telling himself success was within reach. The door swung open and he was thankful his lungs were full of air. His girl was a freaking knockout. "There has never been a more beautiful woman in the history of the world." He pushed the flowers in her direction and was relieved when she took them. A nervous smile curved her full lips and his gut settled just a little. Perhaps he wasn't the only one who had a stomach full of nerves.

Killer trotted into the house and they both let out a laugh simultaneously. "Believe it or not, we talked about manners before arriving."

"Bella and I are not offended by enthusiasm." She trailed her finger over the petal of one of the peonies. "It's one of our favorite things."

"That's good news all around because both the dog and I have a ton of it." He held out his hand. "You ready for our date?"

"Let me just grab my purse."

"You won't need it; we're not going far." A look of disappointment crossed her face, and he told himself it wouldn't remain there long. Once she saw what was in store, she'd likely have nothing but smiles and kind words.

At least he hoped that's what happened.

"Okay, Zane." She set the flowers on the entry table and then took his hand. "You look handsome, by the way."

He led her across the yard. "How you say those words with a straight face, I'll never know."

"I see the whole you and not just a couple of scars on your cheek." She swung their hands. "I thought you were handsome from the moment we met and that hasn't changed. A person's attractiveness is the sum of their heart, mind and soul, not individual bits and pieces."

"I think your kindness colors your perception, but I'm not going to argue the point. The fact that you still have any goodwill to throw in my direction is a damn miracle, and I'm just gonna enjoy it."

"A wise choice."

The Ferris wheel came into view, and he heard Olivia let out a little gasp. "I hope you like the details, I added." He watched her eyes crawl over the fairy lights he'd threaded through the wheel, along with the ribbons he'd attached to the gondolas. Was her awestruck expression a good sign? "You ready for your first ride?"

"But don't you remember…I have a height thing."

"Not a problem, babe. I've got you covered."

"Really? Are you sure?"

"One hundred percent." He bent down and kissed her cheek. "You can trust me."

"I hope so," she muttered as she followed him to a pink gondola.

Zane opened the door with a flourish and helped Olivia in. He plucked two thermoses out of the picnic basket that sat on a large plaid blanket and then climbed into the gondola. "Once we've christened the ride properly, we can have supper."

"And how do you define christen, sir?"

He threw her a wink and closed the door behind him. "I guess that depends on how much you like what I'm about to say." He handed her the pink thermos. "Any and all kind gestures will be accepted with gratitude."

"Interesting," she said, taking the thermos.

He pulled his phone out and hit the playlist Linc had made for him. Music filled the yard, and he watched Olivia move closer. "How are you doing?"

"Nervous."

He took her hand. "Liv, I would never put you in danger."

"I know."

"Do you?"

"Yes," she said quietly.

"Good because here we go." He pushed the amusement ride icon on his phone and heard the engine stir to life. He uncapped her thermos and then did the same with his own. "Here's to making your dreams come true."

Olivia took a gulp and then smiled. "My favorite wine, how perfect."

"Figured having you as relaxed as possible was a good idea." The gondola rose slowly off the ground, and Olivia moved closer, digging her fingers into his. When they were about four feet in the air, it stopped gently.

"Is that it?" she asked, looking over the side of the carriage.

"Yep. I figured it was about all the thrill you could take. If need be, you can jump out and not risk injury."

She let out a strangled laugh. "Holy moly, is the speech you're about to give me going to be that bad?"

"I hope not."

"This is perhaps one of the best surprises I've ever had." She took a long drink and then looked across the yard. "I didn't think you had a romantic bone in your whole body."

"Seems I have quite a few." He kissed the top of her head, feeling his heart do some sort of strange tango. "I knew this idea had a fifty-fifty chance of going sideways. I'm relieved that you trusted me enough to give it a shot."

Olivia peered over the side and sucked in a breath. "I kinda like it up here."

"Want to go a little higher?" He held up his phone with a wide smile.

"No thanks." She gave him a jaunty wink. "I may still need to jump out."

"Fair enough." He slid his arm over her shoulder. "I'm sorry, Liv."

"For what?"

"Giving you mixed messages about my interest, vacillating between all in and running away." He traced her hand. "I'm talking to a therapist twice a week now and am committed to my mental health."

"That's the best news, Zane. You deserve all the good that comes your way. Forgiving yourself and evicting those bad old demons is going to make that possible."

"Thanks, babe." He let gratitude fill his chest and did as his therapist instructed, and simply sat with the good feeling. "Do you think giving me a second chance is possible somewhere down the road?"

"What exactly do you want a chance...at?"

Hearing the uncertainty in her voice made his heart pinch. Didn't she realize that she was his one and shot at happiness? "Everything." He tightened his hold. "I want it all."

"Define *all*."

"I'd like to start with dating." A disgruntled sigh competed with the sound of the music. "I have a lot to learn about how to be in a relationship successfully. There is a ton of work to do and I'm hoping..." he looked down and told himself the tilt of her mouth was a good sign, "you'll be patient while I figure things out."

"I have some work to do too." She looked up. "You weren't wrong when you called me on my reluctance to go all in." Breathing slowly, she ran her finger over the thermos. "I have my own set of fears that need to be processed."

Peace flooded his system and he couldn't remember the last time he'd felt it. If ever. "What say, we do the hard stuff together and give this thing a shot?"

Olivia took a gulp of wine and then another. "Well...I guess..."

He dipped his head. "Is that a yes to being my girlfriend or a strong maybe?"

She pushed her lips together. "It's a yes, Zane."

Seeing the love in her beautiful eyes made his once shriveled heart expand to twice its size. "I can't sing, write sonnets, or even cook you a decent meal, but I can fix things." He pressed a small kiss to her mouth. "I started with the Ferris wheel and hope to end with mending the crack I made in your heart."

"Your brother said you had a knack for taking things apart and making them better; maybe that's what you're about to do for me."

"I've fallen for you, Liv. And I want...I hope that someday I can have the privilege of holding a piece of your heart."

She looked up. "Silly man, you already do."

His heart tried to beat its way out of his chest and he told himself he deserved happiness. "Good! And know that I plan on showing you every day that the fiercest part of me will always protect the softest part of you."

Pulling him close, she kissed him firmly. "And to think, I didn't even have to put a spell on you."

"Babe, you cast your magic the minute we met. There is no more you and me...only an *us*."

"That's the best kind of news since I'm going to do my best to love you without a single string attached."

"It's you and me from here on out."

"And the dogs," she added before crawling into his lap.

"Of course." The gondola swayed with the weight shift, and he laughed when she scrabbled closer. "Don't worry, babe, I got you."

"You better," she squeaked.

"Trust me. I don't plan on ever letting go."

And he meant it. He was all in and planned to show her what that meant for the rest of their days.

## Epilogue

Zane discovered that once he stopped resisting the inevitable, a relationship wasn't all that hard.

It helped that Olivia was easy to love. She embraced him with a messy heart, and he kissed her with bruised lips.

She listened to his words. And to his silence. "Come here," she would say with her arms held open. And he did because there was no better place in the world.

"Stay," she would command. And he finally did. Because any life without her was not one he was interested in.

She embraced him with fragile confidence, and he touched her with scarred fingers.

They were well aware of the other's flaws and did their best to inhale the storm together.

No more running from happiness. No more avoiding the person that could give life meaning.

Trust.

Zane had finally learned how. And found someone worthy of it.

The woman at the end of Lady Bug Lane saved him.

"Zane…"

"Yeah, babe?"

"You coming?"

"Of course." Pushing open the screen door, he strode across the damp grass and took his wife's outstretched hand.

He'd somehow found the love he needed even though he'd been convinced he needed none.

It seemed God had decided he was worthy of a miracle after all.

Dear reader,
I've included several tantalizing tidbits about
future stories, so if you'd like to see what I'm cooking
up, head over to www.leahartauthor.com.

TEMPTED

LEA HART

TROUBLE

LEA HART

TWISTED

LEA HART

If you'd like a glimpse of Birch in action he's featured in *PATRIOT*, and his tale of love will be published next year.

TANGLED

LEA HART

If you're intrigued by the Colt Hawker, you can meet him in *FASCINATED*. His story will be included in the Coronado Series next year.

CAPTIVATED

WWW.LEAHARTAUTHOR.COM

LEA
HART

# MILITARY ROMANCE
*Witty, hot & delicious*

Come see what happens when hella-hot Navy SEALs
meet their match.
Delicious alpha hero? *Check.* A story sweet
enough to make you swoon? *Also check!*
Smokin' hot love cranked up to a hundred?
*Check and check!*

## CORONADO SERIES
LATCHED
SNATCHED
ATTACHED
CATCH
SERENDIPITY
KISMET
FATE
BEWITCHED
HITCHED

SWITCHED
TUMULT
INFATUATED
FASCINATED
COMPLICATED (2021)

# ROMANTIC ADVENTURE
*Narrow escapes and naughty shenanigans*

Romantic Adventure at its sexy best.
**Come see what happens when bullets fly along
with a few inhibitions.**

## SAI SERIES
### VORTEX
### WHIRLWIND
### TEMPEST
### BESIEGE
### BARRAGE

## A WHOLE LOTTA TROUBLE

## DIRTY SERIES
### DECEIT
### DUPLICITY
### DOUBLE-CROSS
### DIRTY DEAL
### DEVOTION